Praise for

"Steven Erikson is an extraordinary writer. . . . My advice to anyone who might listen to me is: treat yourself."
—Stephen R. Donaldson

"This masterwork of the imagination may be the high-water mark of epic fantasy."
—Glen Cook

"A multilayered tale of magic and war, loyalty and betrayal. Complexly drawn characters occupy a richly detailed world in this panoramic saga."
—*Library Journal*

"Erikson brings a punchy, mesmerizing writing style into the genre of epic fantasy, making an indelible impression."
—Elizabeth Haydon

"Erikson [has a] particular combination of lush description, sharp dialogue, and fantastical, grand imagination."
—*Publishers Weekly*

"Wondrous voyages, demons, and gods abound . . . dense and complex . . . ultimately rewarding."
—*Locus*

Also by Steven Erikson

The Devil Delivered and Other Tales
This River Awakens
*Willful Child**

THE MALAZAN BOOK OF THE FALLEN
Gardens of the Moon
Deadhouse Gates
Memories of Ice
House of Chains
Midnight Tides
The Bonehunters
Reaper's Gale
Toll the Hounds
Dust of Dreams
The Crippled God

Forge of Darkness
*Fall of Light**

Bauchelain and Korbal Broach
Crack'd Pot Trail

*forthcoming

STEVEN ERIKSON

The
Wurms
of
Blearmouth

A Malazan Tale of Bauchelain and Korbal Broach

TOR®

A TOM DOHERTY ASSOCIATES BOOK

NEW YORK

THE WURMS OF BLEARMOUTH

Copyright © 2012 by Steven Erikson

A Tor Book
Published by Tom Doherty Associates, LLC
175 Fifth Avenue
New York, NY 10010

www.tor-forge.com

Tor® is a registered trademark of Tom Doherty Associates, LLC.

The Library of Congress Cataloging-in-Publication Data is available upon request.

ISBN 978-0-7653-2426-9 (hardcover)
ISBN 978-0-7653-7622-0 (trade paperback)
ISBN 978-1-4668-6070-4 (e-book)

Tor books may be purchased for educational, business, or promotional use. For information on bulk purchases, please contact Macmillan Corporate and Premium Sales Department at 1-800-221-7945, extension 5442, or write special markets@macmillan.com.

First published in Great Britain by PS Publishing Ltd.

First U.S. Edition: July 2014

Printed in the United States of America

0 9 8 7 6 5 4 3 2 1

The
Wurms
of
Blearmouth

"Behold!" Arms spread wide and braced against the wind, Lord Fangatooth Claw the Render paused and glanced back at Scribe Coingood. "See how this bold perch incites me to declamation, Scribe?" His narrow, hawkish features darkened. "Why are you not writing?"

Scribe Coingood wiped a drip from his nose, worked his numb fingers for a moment, and then scratched out the one word onto the tablet. Here atop the high tower, it was so cold that the wax on the tablet had chipped and flaked beneath the polished bone point of his scribe. He could barely make out the word he had just written, and the biting ice in his eyes didn't help matters. Squinting against the buffeting wind, he hunched down, pulling tighter his furs, but that did nothing to ease his shivering.

He cursed his own madness that had brought him to West Elingarth's Forgotten Holding. He also cursed this insane sorcerer for whom he now worked. He cursed this rotting keep and its swaying tower. He cursed the town below: Spendrugle of Blearmouth was a hovel, its population cowering under the tyranny of its new lord. He cursed the abominable weather of this jutting spur of land, thrashed by the wild ocean on three sides on most days, barring those times when the wind swung round to howl its way down from the north, cutting across the treeless blight that stretched inland all the way to yet another storm-wracked ocean, six days distant. He cursed his mother, and the time when he was seven and looked in on his sister's room and saw things—oh, what was the point? There were plenty of reasons a man had to curse, and with infernal intimacy he knew most of them.

His dreams of wealth and privilege had suffered the fate of a lame hare on the Plain of Wolves, chewed up and torn to bits; and the wind had long since taken away those tattered remnants: the tufts of blood-matted fur, the wisps of white throat-down, and the well-gnawed splinters of bone. All of it gone, scattered across the blasted landscape of his future.

Chewing on the end of his graver, Coingood considered setting that description down in his secret diaries. *A lame hare on the Plain of Wolves. Yes, that's me all right . . . was that me or my dreams, that hare? Never mind, it's not like there's a difference.* Not when he was huddled here atop the tower, miserably subject to his lord's whim, and Hood knew, a manic, eye-gleaming whim it was.

"Have you written it down now, Scribe? Gods below, if I'd known you were so slow I would never have hired you! Tell me, what did I say? I've forgotten. Read it back, damn you!"

"M-m-master, y'said . . . er . . . 'Behold!'"

"Is that it? Didn't I say anything more?"

"S-s-something 'bout a bold p-p-perch, M-m-milord."

Lord Fangatooth waved one long-fingered, skeletal hand. "Never mind that. I've told you about my asides. They're just that. Asides. Where was I?"

"'Behold!'"

The lord faced outward again, defiant against the roaring seas, and struck a pose looming ominously over the town. "Behold! Oh, and note my widespread arms as I face this wild, whore-whipped sea. Oh, and that wretched town directly below, and how it kneels quivering like an abject slave. Note, too, the grey skies, and that fierce colour of . . . grey. What else? Fill the scene, fool!"

Coingood started scratching furiously on the tablet.

Watching him, Fangatooth made circular, tumbling motions with one hand. "More! Details! We are in the throes of creativity here!"

"I b-b-beg you, m-m-milord, I'm j-j-just a s-s-scribe, n-n-not a poet!"

"Anyone who can write has all the qualifications necessary for artistic genius! Now, where was I? Oh, right. Behold!" He fell silent, and after a long, quivering moment, he slowly lowered his arms. "Well," he said. "That will do for now. Go below, Scribe, and stoke up the fires and the implements of torture. I feel in need of a visit to my beloved brother."

Coingood hobbled his way to the trapdoor.

"Next time I say 'Behold!'," Fangatooth said behind him, "don't interrupt!"

"I w-w-won't, M-m-milord. P-p-promise!"

"There he was again!" Felittle hissed through chattering teeth. "You seen him too, didn't you? Say you did! It wasn't just me! Up on that tower, arms out to the sides, like a . . . like a . . . like a mad sorcerer!"

Spilgit Purrble, deposed Factor of the Forgotten Holding yet still trapped in the town of Spendrugle of Blearmouth, at least until winter's end, peered across at the young woman now struggling to close the door to his closet-sized office. Snow had melted and then refrozen across the threshold. He'd need to take a sword to that at least one more time, so that he could officially close up for the season and retreat back to the King's Heel. As it was, his last day maintaining any kind of office for the backstabbing mob ruling the distant capital and, ostensibly, all of Elingarth, promised to be a cold one.

Even the arrival of Felittle, here in these crowded confines, with her soft red cheeks and the overdone carmine paint on her full lips, and those huge eyes so expansive in their blessed idiocy, could do little to defeat the insipid icy draught pouring in past her from around the mostly useless door. Spilgit sighed and reached for his tankard. "I've warmed rum in that kettle, mixed with some wine and crushed blackgem berries. Would you like some?"

"Ooh!" She edged forward, her quilted coat smelling of smoke, ale and her mother's eye-watering perfume that Spilgit privately called *Whore Sweat*—not that he'd ever utter that out loud. Not if he wanted to get what he wanted from this blissful child in a woman's body. And most certainly never to that vicious hag's face. While Felittle's mother already despised him, she'd not yet refused his coin and he needed to keep it that way for a few more months, assuming he could find a way of stretching his fast-diminishing resources. After that . . .

Felittle was breathing fast as Spilgit collected the kettle from its hook above the brazier and poured out a dollop into the cup she'd taken down from the shelf beside the door. He considered again the delicious absence of guilt that accompanied his thoughts of stealing Felittle away from her tyrant of a mother; away from this miserable village that stank of fish all summer and stank of the people eating that fish all winter; away from her mother's whores and the sordid creatures that crawled into the King's Heel every day eager for more of the old wick-dipping from that gaggle of girls only a blind man would find attractive, at least until the poor fool's probing fingers broke through the powdery sludge hiding their pocked faces. Away, then, and away most of all, from that deranged sorcerer who'd usurped his own brother to carve out, in broken bones, spilled blood and the screaming of endless victims, his private version of paradise.

Oh, there was no end to the horrors of this place, but Lord Fangatooth Claw sat atop them all like a king on a throne. How Spilgit hated sorcerers!

"You're still shivering, darling," he said to Felittle. "Drink that down and have another, and come closer. Now, with only this one chair, well, sit on my lap again, will you. That's surely one way to get warm."

She giggled, swinging her not-ungenerous backside onto him and then leaning back with one arm snaking round the back of his neck. "If Mother saw this, she'd hack off your mast and roast it on a fire till it was burnt crisp!"

"But my sweetheart, are we not dressed? Is this not entirely proper, given the cold and the cramped conditions of this office?"

"Oh, and who else do you do this with?"

"No one, of course, since you are the only person to ever visit me."

She eyed him suspiciously, but he knew it to be an act, since she well knew that he entertained only her. Felittle missed nothing in this village. She was its eyes and ears and, most of all, its mouth, and it was remarkable to Spilgit that such a mouth could find fuel to race without surcease day after day, night upon night. There were barely two hundred people in Spendrugle, and not one of them could be said to be leading exciting lives. Perhaps there was a sort of cleverness in Felittle, after all, in the manner of her soaking in everything that it was possible to know in Spendrugle, and then spewing it all back out with impressive accuracy. *Indeed, she might well possess the wit to match a . . . a . . .*

"Blackgem berries make me squirt, you know."

"Excuse me?"

"Squirt water, of course! What else would I squirt? What a dirty mind you have!"

... *sea-sponge?* "Well, I didn't know that. I mean, how could I, since it's such a . . . well, a private thing."

"Not for much longer," she said, taking another mouthful.

Spilgit frowned, only now feeling the unusual warmth in his lap. "You call that a squirt?"

"Well," she said, "it's just that it got me all excited!"

"Really? Oh, then should we—"

"Not you, silly! Fangatooth! On the tower, with his arms spread wide like I said!"

"Alas, I didn't see any of that, Felittle. Busy as I was in here, putting things in order and all. Even so, for the life of me I can't see what it was that excited you about such a scene. He does that most mornings, after all."

"I know that, but this morning it was different. Or at least I thought it was."

"Why?"

"Well," she paused to drink down the rum, gusted out a sweet sigh, and then made a small sound. "Oop, it's all going now, isn't it?"

Spilgit felt the heat spreading in his crotch, and then his thighs as it pooled in the chair. "Ah, yes . . ."

"Anyway," she continued, "I thought he was looking at the wreck, you see? But I don't think he was. I mean—"

"Hold on, darling. A moment. What wreck?"

"Why, the one in the bay, of course! Arrived last night! You don't know anything!"

"Survivors?"

She shrugged. "Nobody's been down to look yet. Too cold."

"Gods below!" Spilgit pushed her from his lap. He rose. "I need to change."

"You look like you peed yourself! Hah hah!"

He studied her for a moment, and then said, "We're heading down, darling. To that wreck."

"Really? But we'll freeze!"

"I want to see it. You can come with me, Felittle, or you can run back to your ma."

"I don't know why you two hate each other. She only wants what's best for me. But I want to do what her girls do, and why not? It's a living, isn't it?"

"You're far too beautiful for that," Spilgit said.

"That's what she says!"

"And she's right, on that we're agreed. The thing we don't agree on is what your future is going to look like. You deserve better than this horrible little village, Felittle. She'd as much as chain you down if she thought she could get away with it. It's all about her, what she wants you to do for her. Your ma's getting old, right? Needing someone to take care of her, and she'll make you a spinster if you let her."

Her eyes were wide, her breaths coming fast. "Then you'll do it?"

"What?"

"Steal me away!"

"I'm a man of my word. Come the spring, darling, we'll swirl the sands, flatten the high grasses and flee like the wind."

"Okay, I'll go with you!"

"I know."

"No, down to the wreck, silly!"

"Right, my little sea-sponge. Wait here, then. I need go back to the Heel and change . . . unless you need to do the same?"

"No, I'm fine! If I go back Ma will see me and find something for me to do. I'll wait here. I wasn't wearing knickers anyway."

Well, that explains it, doesn't it. Oh darling, you're my kind of woman.

Except for the peeing bit, that is.

The hand gripping his cloak collar was hard as iron as he was dragged from the foaming, icy surf. Hacking, spitting out seawater and sand, Emancipor Reese opened his eyes to stare up at a grey, wintry sky. He heard gulls but couldn't see them. He heard the war-drums of the waves pounding the rocks flanking this slip of a bay. He heard his own phlegmatic gasping, punctuated by the occasional groan as that hand continued dragging him up the beach, across heaps of shells, through snarled knots of seaweed, and over sodden lumps of half-frozen driftwood.

He flailed weakly, clawing at that hand, and a moment later it released him. His head fell back with a thump and he found himself staring up at his master's upside-down face.

"Will you recover, Mister Reese?"

"No, Master."

"Very good. Now get up. We must take stock of our surroundings."

"It's made up of air, not water. That's enough of the surroundings I need to know."

"Nonsense, Mister Reese. We seem to have lost Korbal Broach, and I could use your assistance in finding him."

At that, Emancipor Reese sat up, blinking the rime from his eyes. "Lost? Korbal's lost? Really? He must be dead. Drowned—"

"No, nothing so dire, I'm sure," Bauchelain replied, brushing sand from his cloak.

"Oh." Emancipor found himself staring at the wreck

of the ship. There wasn't much left. Fragments were being tossed up to roll in the surf. "What is it about me and
the sea?" he muttered. Amidst the flotsam were more
than a few bodies, their only movement coming from the
water that pushed and pulled at their limp forms. "It's a
miracle we survived that, Master."

"Mister Reese? Oh, that. Not a miracle at all. Will-
power and fortitude. Now, I believe I spied a settlement
upon the headland, one that includes a rather substan-
tial fortification."

"No," moaned Emancipor, "not another fortification."

"Prone to draughts, I'm sure, but more suited to our
habits. We shall have to introduce ourselves to the local
lord or lady, I think, and gauge well the firmness of his
or her footing. Command, Mister Reese, is a state of
being to which I am not only accustomed, but one for
which my impressive talents are well-suited. That said,
and given our record thus far when assuming positions
of authority, even I must acknowledge that trial and error
remains an important component to our engagement
with power."

"Now here's a miracle," said Emancipor as he pulled
out his pouch of rustleaf. "The hawker claimed it would
be watertight, and she was right." He found his pipe, blew
the wet and sand from it and began tamping the bowl.
"Life's looking up already, Master."

"The lightening of your spirits is most welcome, Mister Reese."

"Show me a man who can't smoke and you're looking at the end of civilization."

"I'll not argue with that assessment, Mister Reese."

The crescent beach they'd found banked steeply above the waterline, and high ragged cliffs rose beyond, but Emancipor could make out a trail. "There's a way up, Master."

"So I see, and if I'm not mistaken, we will find our companion in yonder village."

"He didn't wait for us?"

"He elected wings to effect his escape from the sinking ship, Mister Reese. I would have done the same, if not for you."

"Ah. Appreciate that, Master. I really do."

"My pleasure. Now— Oh, we have company on the way."

Emancipor saw, too, the three figures making their way down the trail, hunched over against the buffeting wind. "Are they armed, Master? This could be a wreckers' coast."

"Armed?"

"My eyes ain't what they used to be, Master."

"No, Mister Reese. Not excessively so. I assure you, to us they pose no danger."

"Glad to hear it, Master." Emancipor was starting to get cold, or, rather, he was starting to feel it. His dunk in the seas had numbed things up pretty fast. Glancing over at Bauchelain, he saw that the tall necromancer was not even wet. Mages, he concluded, were obnoxious in so many ways it was almost pointless listing them.

Now shivering, he studied the three strangers making their way down the trail.

Hordilo Stinq's pirating days were behind him now. He liked the feel of solid ground under him, even as that terrible sea still held him close, within reach, stubborn as an ex-wife whose sole reason to breathe was the conviction that she was still owed something by the fool she'd tossed away, and it didn't matter how many years had passed since he'd last wallowed in her icy arms. The watery witch never let him wander too far from her thrashing shores. These days, it was nothing to step outside to begin his daily patrol, and feel on the wind the wet spray of her bitter spite. Aye, an ex-wife, spitting like a cat and howling like a dog. A hoary, wild thing with venom under her long nails and dead spiders in her hair.

"You ain't answered me, Stinq," said Ackle, who sat across from him and was, thankfully, not looking Hordilo's way, busy instead plucking clumps of old mud from his deadman's cloak. "Ever been married?"

"No," Hordilo replied. "Nor do I want to be, Ackle. Want no ex-wives chasing me down everywhere I go, throwing snotty runts at my feet I never seen before and sayin' they're mine. When they aren't. I mean, if my seed produced anything as ugly as that—well, gods below, I've known plenty of women, if you know what I mean, and not one of them ever called me ugly."

Ackle paused, examining a long root he'd pulled from the woolen cloak. "Heard you like Rimlee," he said. "She can't see past her nose."

"Your point?"

"Nothing, friend. Just that she's mostly blind. That's all."

Hordilo drained his tankard and glared out through the thick, pitted glass of the window. "Feloovil's whores ain't selected for how good they look—see, I mean. How good they see. But I bet you wish they wasn't the smelling kind, don't you?"

"If they smell I remain unaware of it," Ackle replied.

"That's not what I meant. They smell just fine, and that's your problem, isn't it?"

At that Ackle looked up—Hordilo could see the man's face reflected blurrily, unevenly, in the window, but even this distorted view couldn't hide Ackle's horrible, lifeless eyes. "Is that my problem, Hordilo? Is that why I can't get a woman to lie with me no matter how much I offer to pay? You think so? I mean, my smell turns them, does it? Are you sure about that?"

Hordilo scowled. Out on the street beyond he saw Grimled stump past, making the first circuit of the day. "You don't smell too good, Ackle. Not that you could tell."

"No, I couldn't. I can't. But you know, there's plenty of men in here who don't smell too good, but they get company in their beds upstairs anyway, every night if they can afford it."

"Different kind of smell," Hordilo insisted. "Living smell, if you know what I mean."

"I would think," said Ackle, straightening in his seat, "that my smell is the least of their concerns. I would think," he went on, "that it's more to do with my having been pronounced dead, stuck in a coffin for three days, and then buried for two more. Don't you think it might be all that, Stinq? I don't know, of course. I mean, I can't be sure, but it seems plausible that these details have something to do with my lonely nights. At least, it's a pos-sibility worth considering, don't you think?"

Hordilo shrugged. "You still smell."

"What do I smell like?"

"Like a corpse in a graveyard."

"And have I always smelled that way?"

Hordilo scowled. "How should I know? Probably not. But I can't really say, can I? Since I never knew you before, did I? You washed up on shore, right? And I had a quota to fill and you were broke."

"If you'd let me lead you to the buried chest you'd be rich now," Ackle said, "and I wouldn't have been strung up because your lord likes to see 'em dance. It could've gone another way, Hordilo, if you had any brains in that skull of yours."

"Right. So why don't you lead me to that damned chest you keep talkin' about? It's not like you need the coin anymore, is it? Anyway, the whole point you're avoiding is that we hanged you good, and you was dead when we took you down. Dead people are supposed to stay in the ground. It's a rule."

"If I was dead I wouldn't be sitting here right now, would I? Ever clawed your way up out of the ground? If that coffin lid wasn't just cheap driftwood, and if your ground wasn't so hard and if your gravediggers weren't so damned lazy, why, I would never have made it back. So, if there's anyone to blame for me being here, it's all of you in this lousy village."

"I didn't dig the grave though, did I? Anyway, there ain't no buried chest. If there was, you'd have gone back to it by now. Instead, you sleep under the table, and that only because her dogs like rolling on you to disguise their scent. Feloovil thinks you're funny, besides."

"She laughs at my dead eyes, you mean."

Hordilo glanced into the tavern's main room, but Feloovil was still sitting behind the bar, her head barely visible, her eyes closed. The woman stayed up till dawn most nights, so it was no surprise she slept most of the day every day. He'd watched that useless Factor, Spilgit Purrble, slink past her a while earlier, and she'd not raised a lid, not even when the man returned from his upstairs room only moments later, and wearing a change of clothes. There'd been a suspicious look on the Factor's face that was still nagging Hordilo, but for the moment he didn't feel like moving, and besides, with Feloovil asleep it was no difficult thing to draw the taps for a flagon or two, on the house as it were. "Lucky you," he finally said, "that she's got an uncanny streak in her. Unlucky for you that her girls don't share it, hah."

"With what they must see in a man's eyes every night," said Ackle, "you'd think they'd welcome mine."

"Lust ain't so bad t'look at," Hordilo said.

"Oh indeed. Why, it charms a woman right out of her clothes, doesn't it? I mean, it's just like love, isn't it? Love with all the dreamy veils torn aside."

"What veils? Her girls don't wear veils, you fool. The point is, Ackle, what they see every night is what they're used to, and they're fine with that. Dead eyes, well, that's different. It puts a shiver on the soul, it does."

"And does my reflection in the window keep you warm, Stinq?"

"If I had an ex-wife, she'd probably have your eyes."

"No doubt."

"But I don't need reminding of what I've been lucky enough to avoid all these years. Well, sometimes, but not all the time. I got a limit to what I can stomach, if you get my meaning."

"I get your meaning, Stinq. Well, sometimes, but not all the time, as you're such a subtle man."

Hordilo grunted, and then frowned. Grimled should have been by already, second time around. It was a small village, and doing the circuit was what Grimled did, and did well, since he didn't know how to do it otherwise. "Something funny," he said.

"What?"

"Fangatooth's golem, Grimled."

"What about it?"

"Not 'it.' 'Him.' Anyway, he showed up as usual—"

"Yes, I saw that."

"The rounds, right? Only, he ain't come back."

Ackle shrugged. "Might be sorting something out."

"Grimled don't sort things out," Hordilo replied, squinting and wiping at the steamy glass. "To sort things out, all he has to do is show up. You don't argue with a giant lump of angry iron. Especially one carrying a two-handed axe."

"It's the bucket head that I don't like," said Ackle. "You can't talk to a bucket, can you? Not face-to-face, I mean. There is no face. But that bucket's not iron, Stinq."

"Yes it is."

"Got to be tin, or pewter."

"No, it's iron," said Hordilo. "You don't work with Grimled the way I do."

"Work with it? You salute it when you pass it by. It's not like you're its friend, Stinq."

"I'm the lord's executioner, Ackle. Grimled and his brothers do the policing. It's all organized, right? We work for the Lord of Wurms. It's like the golems are milord's right hands, and I'm the left."

"Right hands? How many does he have?"

"Count it up, fool. Six right hands."

"What about his own right hand?"

"All right. Seven right hands."

"And two left?"

"That's right. I guess even the dead can count, after all."

"Oh, I can count, friend, but that doesn't mean it all adds up, if you understand my meaning."

"No," Hordilo said, glaring at the reflection, "I don't."

"So the bucket's iron. Fine, whatever you say. Grim-led's gone missing and even I will admit: that's passing strange. So, as executioner and constable or whatever it is you say you do, officially, I mean, and let's face it, you chirp something different every second day. So, as whatever you are, why are you still sitting here, when Grim-led's gone missing. It's cold out there. Maybe it rusted up. Or froze solid. Go get yourself a tub of grease. It's what a real friend would do, under the circumstances."

"Just to prove it to you, then," said Hordilo, rising up and tugging on his cloak, "I'll do just that. I'll head out there, into this horrible weather, to check on my com-rade."

"Use a wooden bucket for that grease," said Ackle. "You don't want to insult your friend, do you?"

"I'll just head over to the Kelp carter's first," said Hordilo, nodding as he adjusted his sword belt.

"For the grease."

"That's right. For the grease."

"In case your friend's seized up."

"Yeah, what is it with these stupid questions?"

Ackle held up two dirt-stained palms, leaning back. "Ever since I died, or, rather, didn't die, but should've, I've acquired this obsession with being . . . well, precise.

I have an aversion to vague generalities, you see. That grey area, understand? You know, like being stuck between certain ideas, important ideas, that is. Between say, breathing and not breathing. Or being alive and being dead. And things like needing to know how many hands Lord Fangatooth has, which by my count is seven right hands and two left hands, meaning, I suppose, that he rarely gets it wrong."

"What in Hood's name are you going on about, Ackle?"

"Nothing, I suppose. It's just that, well, since we're friends, you and me, I mean. As much as you're friends with Grimled . . . well, what I'm saying is, this cold slows me up something awful, I've found. Maybe I don't need grease, as such, but if you see me out there sometime, not moving or anything. I guess the point I'm making, Stinq, is this. If you see me like that, don't bury me."

"Because you ain't dead? You idiot. You couldn't be more dead than you are now. But I won't bury you. Burn you on a pyre, maybe, if only to put an end to our stupid conversations. So take that as a warning. I see you all frozen up out there, you're cordwood in my eyes and that's all."

"So much for friendship."

"You got that right. I ain't friends with a dead man I don't even know."

"No, just lumps of magicked iron with buckets for heads."

"Right. At least we got that straight." Hordilo pushed the chair back and walked over to the door. He paused and glanced back to see Ackle staring out the window. "Hey, look somewhere else. I don't want your dead eyes tracking me."

"They may be dead," Ackle replied with a slow smile, "but they know ugly when they see it."

Hordilo stared at the man. "You remind me," he said, "of my ex-wife."

Comber Whuffine Gaggs lived in a shack just above the comber's beach. He'd built it himself, using driftwood and detritus from the many wrecks he'd plundered as lost traders struck the sunken reefs that were noted only on the rarest of maps with the grim label of *Gravewater*, and which the locals called *Sunrise Surprise*. Indeed, the night storms on this headland were nasty, bloodthirsty, vengeful, cold and cruel as a forgotten mistress, and he'd made his home a doorstep from which he could view her nightly tirades, wetting his lips in the hope of something new and wonderful arriving in splintered ruin and faint, hopeless cries.

But it was a cold squat, here above the beach, the wooden walls gritted in the cracks and polished like bone by the winds, and so he'd made of those walls two layers, with a cavity in between into which, over the course of three decades, he'd stuffed the cuttings from his scalp and beard.

The smell of that stuffing was, admittedly, none too pleasant to the guest or stranger who paid him a visit, if only to look over the loot he'd scrounged up from the wrack, and such visits had become increasingly rare, forcing him to load up his handcart for the morning market that sprang up in Spendrugle's centre square every few weeks or so. That journey both exhausted him and left him feeling depressed; and it wasn't often that he came back at the day's end with anything more than a handful of the tooth-dented coins of tin that passed for local currency.

No, these days he was inclined to stay at home, especially now that a mad sorcerer had taken over the Holding, and strangers had a way of ending up with a hanged-man's view of the scenic sites that made Spendrugle such a charming village. So rare had his visits become he truly feared that one day he might be mistaken for one of those hapless strangers.

He'd heard the ship come in this past night, striking the reef like a legless horse sliding across a dhenrabi's bristling hide, but the morning had broken unruly cold, and he knew that he had plenty of time in which to explore, once the sun climbed a little higher and the wind whipped back round.

The lone room of his shack was bright and warm with a half-dozen ship's lanterns, all lit up and hissing from the occasional drop of old rain making its way down through the roof's heavy, tarred beams. He was perched on the edge of an old captain's chair, its leather padding salt-stained but otherwise serviceable, and sat leaning far forward to make sure every hair he scraped off his jaw and cheeks, and every strand he clipped from his head, fell down to the bleached deerskin he'd laid out between his feet. He had been mulling notions of adding a room . . .

It was then that he heard voices drifting up from the beach. Survivors were rare, what with the rocks offshore and the deadly undertow and all. Whuffine set down his blade and collected up a cloth to wipe the soap from his face. It was simple decency to head down and offer up a welcome, maybe even a cup of warmed rum to take the chill from their bones, and then with a smile send them on their way to Spendrugle, so Hordilo could arrest them and see them hung high. It wasn't much by way of local entertainment, but he could think of worse.

Like me, dangling there beneath the overhang atop Wurms' stone wall, with the gulls fighting over my tender bits. No, he wouldn't find that entertaining at all.

Besides, delivering such hapless fools had its rewards, as Hordilo gave him the pickings from whatever they happened to be wearing and carrying, and the fine high leather boots he now pulled on reminded him of that, making this venture out into the bitter cold feel worthwhile. He rose from the chair and drew on his sheepskin cloak, which was made of four hides all sewn together in such a way that the heads crowded his shoulders and the hind legs hung like dirty braids past his hips. He'd been a big man, once, but the years had withered his muscles, so that now his frame was all jutting bones and stringy tendons, wrapped up in skin like chewed leather. He didn't have many tender bits left, but he knew the damned gulls would find them, given the chance.

Pulling on his fox-fur hat, made of two skins with the heads hanging down to protect his ears, and the bushy tails pulled into a warm fringe round the crown of his dented skull, he gathered up his knobby walking stick and set out.

The instant he emerged from his shack he halted in surprise to see two bent-over figures hurrying down the trail. A man and a woman. Gaze narrowing on the man, Whuffine called out, "Is that you?"

Both villagers looked up.

"Why, I'm always me," Spilgit Purrble said. "Who else would I be, old man?"

Whuffine scowled. "I ain't as old as I look, you know."

"Stop," said Spilgit, "you're breaking my heart. I see you're getting ready for a day of picking through bloated corpses."

But Whuffine was studying the sands of the trail. "See anybody on your way down?" he asked.

"No," said the woman. "Why?"

Whuffine glanced at her. "You're Feloovil's daughter, ain't you? Does she know you're here? With him?"

"Look," said Spilgit, "we're going down for a look. You coming or not?"

"That's my beach down there, Factor."

"The whole village takes its share," Spilgit countered.

"Because I let them, because I've been through everything first." He then shook his head, making the fox heads flap and the sharp canines run eerily along his neck—he shouldn't have left in the upper jaws, probably. "Anyway, look at the ground here, you two. Someone's come up the trail—Hood knows how I didn't hear that, or even see it, since I was at the window. And if that's not enough, there's more."

"More what?" Spilgit asked.

"Whoever it was passing me and my shack, it was dragging bodies. Two of 'em, one to each hand. Makes for a strong person, don't you think? This trail's steep and dragging things up all this way ain't easy."

"We didn't see anyone," Spilgit said.

Whuffine then pointed down towards the beach. "I just heard voices below."

Felittle gasped. "We should go and get Hordilo!"

"No need," said Whuffine. "I was going to send them up, anyway. It's what I do."

Spilgit spat but the wind shifted and the spittle whipped up and plastered his brow. Cursing, he wiped it away and said, "You all have blood on your hands, don't you? That tyrant up in the keep found himself the right people to rule over, all right."

"You're just saying that," said Whuffine, "because you're sore. What's it like, eh? Being made useless and all?"

"That's a usurper up there in Wurms."

"So what? His brother was, too. And that witch before him, and then that bastard son of Lord Wurms himself— who strangled the man in his own bed. And what was he even doing in that bed with his stepfather anyway?"

Whuffine shrugged. "It's how them fools do things, and us, why, we just got to keep our heads down and get on with living and all. You, Spilgit, you're just a Hood-damned tax collector anyway. And we ain't paying and that's that."

"I don't care," Spilgit said, taking Felittle's arm and pulling her along as he trudged past Whuffine. "I quit. And when the Black Fleet shows up and an army lands to bring down in flames Wurms Keep and that mad sorcerer with it, well, I don't expect there'll be much left of Spendrugle of Blearmouth either, and the gods of mercy will be smiling on that day!"

During this tirade, voiced as Spilgit marched on, Whuffine fell in behind the two villagers. He thought about pushing past them both, but with living people on the beach, maybe it paid to be cautious. "Anyway," he said, "why are you two going down there, now that you know there's survivors? You ain't going to warn them off or anything, are you? If you did that, why, Hordilo and Lord Fangatooth himself wouldn't take kindly to that. In fact, they'd have to find somebody else to hang."

Ahead, Spilgit paused and swung round. "I'm surviving one more winter here, Whuffine. You think I'd do or say anything to jeopardize that?"

"I like the hangings," said Felittle, offering Whuffine a bright, cock-stirring smile. "But aren't you curious? How did anyone survive that storm? They might come from mysterious places! They might have funny hair and funny clothes and talk in gibberish! It's so exciting, isn't it?"

Whuffine flicked a glance at Spilgit, but couldn't read much from the man's expression, other than the fact that he was shivering. To Felittle, Whuffine smiled back and said, "Aye, exciting."

"Aren't you cold?" she asked him. "You don't look cold. How come you're not cold?"

"It's my big kindly heart, lass."

"Gods below," Spilgit said, swinging round and pulling Felittle with him.

They rounded the last bend in the trail and came within sight of the beach. And there on the pale strand stood two men, one tall and dressed in fine clothing— black silks and black leathers, and a heavy burgundy woolen cloak that reached down almost to his ankles— and beside him a more bedraggled figure, a man Whuffine guessed was a sailor by the rough clothes he wore and the way he stood on those bowed legs. Beyond these two, the surf was crowded with corpses and detritus. Out on the reef the wreck had already been battered to pieces, with barely a third of the hull remaining, and only the foredeck, over which was wrapped the tangled remnants of a sail that looked partly scorched.

Spilgit and Felittle had both paused upon seeing the strangers, proving once again the pith behind the bluff when it came to that tax collector. Whuffine edged past them and continued down to the strand. "Welcome, friends! Mael and all his hoary whores have looked kindly upon you, I see. To think, you seem to have escaped unscathed from the furies, while your poor companions behind you lie cold and nothing but meat for the crabs. Do you give thanks for such mercy? I'm sure you do!"

The taller man, fork-bearded and with his hair slicked back from his bared head, frowned slightly at Whuffine and then turned to his companion and said something in a language the Comber didn't understand, to which the man grunted and said, "Low Elin, Master. Seatrader tongue. Eastern pirates. Sailor's Cant. It's just the accent that's thrown you. And by that accent, Master, I'd say we've hit the Headland of Howling Winds. Probably the Forgotten Holding, meaning it's claimed by the Enclave." This man then turned to Whuffine. "There's a river other side of the keep, right?"

Whuffine nodded. "The Blear, aye. You know well this shore, then, sir. I'm impressed."

The man grunted a second time and spoke to his companion. "Master, we're on a Wreckers' Coast here. That heap of sheepskin and furs with all his happy words and big smile, he's eager to start stripping corpses and picking through the wrack. See those boots he's wearing? Malazan cavalry officer, and he ain't no Malazan cavalry officer. If we was badly hurt he'd probably have slit our throats by now."

Slipgit laughed, earning a glare from Whuffine, who was struggling to hold onto his smile.

The tall man cleared his throat, and then spoke in passable High Elin. "Well then, let us leave the man to his task, since I doubt our dead comrades will mind. Alas, as we are hale, there will be no throat-slitting just yet."

"The villagers won't be any better," the other man then said, eyeing Spilgit and Felittle.

"Do not be so quick to judge us," Spilgit said, stepping forward. "Until recently, I was the appointed Factor of the Forgotten Holding, and as such the official representative of the Enclave."

The sailor raised his brows at that, and then grinned. "A damned tax collector? Surprised they ain't hanged you yet."

Whuffine saw Spilgit blanch, but before he could say anything, the Comber cleared his throat and said, "The lord is resident in his keep, good sirs." Then, shifting his attention to the taller man, he added, "And he will be delighted to make your acquaintance, seeing as you're highborn and all."

"Is there an inn?" the sailor asked, and Whuffine noted how the man shivered in his sodden clothes.

"Allow us to escort you there," Spilgit said. "This young woman with me is the daughter of the innkeeper."

"Most civilized of you, Factor," said the highborn man. "As you can see, my manservant is suffering in this weather."

"A warm fire and a hearty meal will do him wonders, I'm sure," said Spilgit. "Yet you, sir, appear to be both dry and, well, proof against this bitter wind."

"Very perceptive of you," the man murmured in reply, glancing about as if distracted. A moment later he shrugged and gestured towards the trail. "Lead on, Factor." Then he paused and looked to his manservant. "Mister Reese, if you would, draw your sword and ware our backs, lest this Malazan cavalry officer falter in his wisdom, and do note the knife he hides in his right hand, will you?"

Scowling, Whuffine stepped back, sheathing his knife. "The blade's for swollen fingers, that's all. In fact, I'll be on my way then, and leave you in the hands of Spilgit and Felittle." And he hurried down the beach. He didn't like the look of that highborn or the way the manservant was now handling that shortsword with unpleasant ease, and all things told, Whuffine was glad to be rid of them.

Coming down to the wrack, eyes scanning the corpses, he paused upon seeing the ragged bites taken out of most of them. He'd seen the work of sharks, but that was nothing like what he looked upon now. Despite his sheepskin and fox-furs, Whuffine shivered. Glancing back, he saw Spilgit and Felittle leading the strangers up the trail. *Could be a bit of trouble washed up here today, eh? Well, I doubt Fangatooth and his golems will have anything to worry about. Still . . .* He eyed the nearest, chewed-up corpse. Some of those bites looked human.

The crabs were marching up from the sea in scuttling rows, and through the moaning wind he could hear their happy, eager clicking.

I'll set out the traps once they've fattened up some.

Hordilo Stinq felt Ackle the Risen's dead eyes tracking him as, bucket of whale grease in one hand, he walked up the street opposite the King's Heel. Most strangers did the proper thing and died after being hung, but not Ackle. If Hordilo was a superstitious man, why, he might think there was something odd about that man.

But he had more practical concerns to deal with right now. Adjusting his sword belt with one hand while tightening his grip on the iron handle of the wooden bucket, and doing his best to ignore how the icy wind stole all feeling from his fingers, he set out up the street. The ground was frozen hard, the edges of the wheel ruts slippery and treacherous, the puddles filling those ruts frozen solid. For all of that, Grimled's progress was mapped out before him in cracked impressions, the golem's iron boots leaving dents already leaking turgid water that pretty much froze as soon as it bled out. His gaze tracked them up to the front street's end, where the footprints turned right and disappeared behind Blecker's Livery.

Hordilo continued on. Those damned golems unnerved him. Ackle was right in that one thing, Hood take him. Offering up a nod and maybe a muttered greeting as one trudged past wasn't what anyone in their right mind could call a friendship. But they were Lord Fangatooth's creations, stamp-stamp-stamping his authority on Spendrugle and everyone calling it home, and if any acts of kindness on Hordilo's part, no matter how modest, could alight the glint of sympathy in such abominations, well, he had to try, didn't he? Besides, the few times there'd been trouble with some stranger, one of them would show up to sort things out right quick, and that had saved Hordilo's skin more than once.

So in a way he owed them, didn't he? And if it wasn't

in a walking lump of iron to feel anything about anyone, Hordilo was flesh and blood, with genuine feelings and even a heart that could break if, say, some hag
of a wife he'd once loved went and did the nasty on
him, and not just one animal, either, but all kinds of
animals, and then told him about it with shining eyes
and that soul-cutting half-smile that said she liked what
her words were doing to him and besides, Ribble had
been *his* dog, dammit! If something like that had ever
happened to him, which of course it hadn't, why, his
heart might break, or at least start leaking. Because a
man without feelings was no better than a . . . well, a
golem.

Reaching Blecker's Livery, he paused for a moment to
utter a soft prayer to the memory of old Blecker, since
remorse always came afterwards and never went away,
when the fury of knowing that Blecker knew everything
with his nickering stallion and all, well, that faded after
a time, and that ex-wife he didn't have was a seductive
woman when she wanted to be, not that Ribble cared
much either way, with his endless panting and witless
but knowing eyes, but Blecker himself had seen plenty,
hadn't he, with his damned menagerie and all. But whisper a prayer anyway, because Hordilo knew that that was
what a decent man did, but not much of a prayer, since
Blecker had never known a thing about decency and no-

body had complained much when he swung from the gibbet, except when they saw Hurta riding off on that stallion with Ribble chasing after them, none of them ever to be seen again—oh, there was plenty of disappointment about that, wasn't there? That said, Feloovil had cleared his tab at the Heel and spotted him free drinks for a whole week afterwards, which was peculiarly generous of her. This was the kind of mess having a wife would have given him, and was it any wonder he was having none of that?

Rounding the livery, Hordilo halted in his tracks. Twenty paces away, Grimled was lying motionless on its back. A large black-cloaked man was kneeling beside it, his hands deep in the golem's chest. Strange fluids were spraying out past the man's forearms. A few paces beyond them lay two bloated corpses.

"Hey!" Hordilo shouted.

But the man ripping pieces out from Grimled's chest didn't look up.

Hordilo set down the bucket and then drew his sword. "Hey!" he yelled again, advancing. "What have you done to Grimled? You can't do that! Step away from him! By the lord's command, step away!"

At last, the stranger looked up, blinking owlishly at Hordilo.

Something in the man's piggy eyes made Hordilo

slow down and then stagger to a halt. He lifted the sword threateningly, but the blade wavered in his numbed grip. "The lord of Wurms Keep will see you hang for this! You're under arrest!"

The stranger withdrew his hands from Grimled's chest. They were black and dripping. "I was trying to fix it," he said in a high, piping voice.

"You broke it!"

"I didn't mean to."

"Explain that to Lord Fangatooth! Get up now. You're coming with me."

The stranger's uncanny eyes slipped past Hordilo and fixed on the distant keep. "There?"

"There."

"All right," the man replied, climbing slowly to his feet. He looked over at the two corpses. "But I want to bring my friends with me."

"Your friends? They're dead!"

"No, not those ones."

The man pointed and Hordilo turned to see a group appearing from the beach trail. *That's where Spilgit was going, and Felittle with him! She must have seen a ship on the reef and snuck out to the Factor, so they could get a first look. Gods below, will the treachery never end?*

"But I want these ones, too," added the stranger. "I'm saving them."

44

Licking his lips, his mind in a fog, Hordilo said, "They're past saving, you fool."

The stranger frowned. "I don't like being called a fool."

The tone was flat, unaccountably chilling. "Sorry to tell you, those two are dead. Maybe you're in shock or something. That happens. Shipwreck, was it? Bad enough you arriving uninvited, and if that wasn't enough, look what you did to Grimled. Lord Fangatooth won't be happy about that, but that's between you and him. Me, well, the law says I got to arrest you, and that's that. The law says you got to give account of yourselves."

"My selves? There is only one of me."

"You think you're being funny? You're not." Stepping back, trying to avoid a peek into the inner workings of poor Grimled—not that they worked anymore— Hordilo shifted his attention to the newcomers as they arrived.

The tall one with the pointed beard spoke. "Ah, Korbal, there you are. What have you found?"

"A golem, Bauchelain," the first man replied. "It swung its axe at me. I didn't like that, but I didn't mean to break it."

The man named Bauchelain walked over to study Grimled. "A distinct lack of imagination, wouldn't you say, Korbal? A proper face would have been much more effective, in terms of inspiring terror and whatnot. Instead, what fear is inspired by an upended slop bucket? Unless it is to invite someone to laugh unto death."

"Don't say that, Master," said the third stranger, pausing to tamp more rustleaf into his pipe, though his teeth chattered with the cold. "What with the way I go and all."

"I am sure," said Bauchelain, "that your sense of humour is far too refined to succumb to this clumsy effort, Mister Reese."

"Oh, it's funny enough, I suppose, but you're right, I won't bust a side about it."

Spilgit was almost hopping from one foot to the other behind the newcomers. "Hordilo, best escort these two gentlemen up to an audience with Lord Fangatooth, don't you think? We'll take their manservant to the Heel, so he can warm up and get a hot meal in him. Spendrugle hospitality, and all that."

Hordilo cleared his throat.

But Korbal was the first to speak. "Bauchelain, this man called me a fool."

"Oh dear," said Bauchelain. "And has he not yet retracted his misjudged assessment?"

"No."

"It was all a misunderstanding," Hordilo said, feeling

sudden sweat beneath his clothes. "Of course he's not a fool. I do apologise."

"There," said Bauchelain, sighing.

"I mean," Hordilo went on, "he killed one of the lord's golems. Oh, and he wants to bring those two bodies with him up to the keep, because they're his friends. So, I don't know what he is, to be honest, but I'll allow that he ain't a fool. Lord Fangatooth, of course, might think otherwise, but it's not for me to speak for him on that account. Now, shall we go?"

"Hordilo—" began Spilgit.

"Yes," Hordilo replied, "you can take the manservant, before he freezes solid."

Bauchelain turned to his manservant. "Off with you, then, Mister Reese. We'll summon you later this evening."

Hordilo grunted a laugh.

"All right, Master." Mister Reese then glanced down at Grimled and looked over at Hordilo. "So, how many of these things has your lord got, anyway?"

"Two more," Hordilo replied. "This one was Grimled. The others are Gorebelly and Grinbone."

Mister Reese choked, coughed out smoke. "Gods below, did the lord name them himself?"

"Lord Fangatooth Claw the Render is a great sorcerer," said Hordilo.

"I'm sorry, Lord what?"

"Go on, Mister Reese," ordered Bauchelain. "We can discuss naming conventions at a later time, yes?"

"Conventions, Master? Oh. Of course, why not? All right, Slipgit—"

"That's Spilgit."

"Sorry. Spilgit, lead me to this blessed inn, then."

Hordilo watched them hurry off, his gaze fixing with genuine admiration on Felittle's swaying backside, and then he returned his attention to the two strangers, and raised his sword. "Am I going to need this out, gentlemen? Or will you come along peacefully?"

"We are great believers in peace," said Bauchelain. "By all means, sheathe your sword, sir. We are looking forward to meeting your sorcerer lord, I assure you."

Hordilo hesitated, and then, since he could no longer feel his fingers, he slid his sword back into its scabbard. "Right. Follow me, and smartly now."

Scribe Coingood watched Warmet Humble writhe in his chains. The chamber reeked of human waste, forcing Coingood to hold a scented handkerchief to his nose. But at least it was warm, with the huge three-legged bronze brazier sizzling and crackling and hissing and throwing up sparks every time his lord decided it was time to heat up the branding iron.

Weeping, spasms clawing their way through his broken body that hung so hapless from the chains, Warmet Humble was a sorry sight. This was what came of brotherly disputes that never saw resolution. Misunderstandings escalated, positions grew entrenched; argument fell away into deadly silence across the breakfast table, and before too long one of them ended up drugged and waking up in chains in a torture chamber. Coingood was relieved that he had been an only child, and the few times he'd ended up in chains was just his father teaching him a lesson about staying out after dark or cheating on his letters and numbers. In any case, if he'd had a brother, why, he'd never use a bhederin branding iron on him, which could brand a five year old from toe to head in a single go. Surely an ear-puncher would do; the kind the shepherds used on their goats and sheep.

Poor Warmet's face bore one end of the brand's mark, melted straight across the nose and both cheeks. Fangatooth had then angled it to sear first one ear and then the other. The horrid, red weal more or less divided Warmet's once-handsome face into an upper half and a lower half.

Brothers.

Humming under his breath, Fangatooth stirred the coals. "The effect is lost," he then said, lifting up the branding iron with both hands and a soft grunt and then frowning at the burning bits of flesh snagged on it, "when it is scar tissue being scarred anew. Scribe! Feed my imagination, damn you!"

"Perhaps, milord, a return to something more delicate."

Fangatooth glanced over. "Delicate?"

"Exquisite, milord. Tiny and precise, but excruciatingly painful?"

"Oh, I like that notion. Go on!"

"Fingernails—"

"Done that. Are you blind?"

"They're growing back, milord. Tender and pink."

"Hmm. What else?"

"Strips of skin?"

"He barely has any skin worthy of the name, Scribe. No, that would be pointless."

Warmet ceased his weeping and lifted his head. "I beg you, brother! No more! My mind is snapped, my body ruined. My future is one of terrible pain and torment. My past is memories of the same. My present is an ending howl of agony. I cannot sleep, I cannot rest my limbs—see how my head trembles in the effort to raise it? I beg you, Simplet—"

"That is no longer my name!" shrieked Fangatooth. He stabbed the branding iron into the coals. "I will burn out your tongue for that!"

"Milord," Coingood said, "by your own rules, he must be able to speak, and see and indeed, hear."

"Oh, that! Well, I'm of a mind to change my mind! I can do that, can't I? Am I not the lord of this keep? Do I not command life and death over thousands?"

Well, hundreds, but why quibble? "You do indeed, milord. The world quakes at your feet. The sky weeps, the wind screams, the seas thrash, the very ground beneath us groans."

Fangatooth spun round to face Coingood. "That's good, Scribe. That's very good. Write that down!"

"At once, milord." Coingood collected up his tablet and bone graver. But the heat had melted the wax and he watched the letters fade even as he wrote. This was not a detail, he decided, worth sharing with his master. After all, there was another set of chains in this dungeon, and the wretched figure hanging from them was if anything even closer to death than poor Warmet Humble. A quick look in that direction revealed no motion from that forlorn victim.

Some strangers had arrived and proved too obnoxious to simply hang. For a time then, his lord had taken great pleasure in rushing from one prisoner to the other, and in a foul fug of burning flesh the screams had come from both sides of the chamber, along with spraying fluids that dried brown on the stone walls. But it could not last. Whatever uncanny will to live that was burning in Warmet's soul was evidently unmatched by that other victim in this dungeon. "Done, milord."

"Every word?"

"Every word, milord."

"Very good. Now, take note of this, and in detail. Dear brother, your life is in my hands. I can kill you at any time. I can make you scream, and twist in pain. I can hurt you bad—no, wait. Scratch out that last one, Scribe. Twist in pain. Yes. In agony. Twisting agony. I can make you twist in twisting agony. No! Not that one, either. Give me some more, Scribe. What's wrong with you?"

Coingood thought frantically. "You've covered it well, milord—"

"No! There must be more! Burn, pull, cut, impale, kick, slap. Slap? Yes, slap slap slap!" And Fangatooth walked up to his brother and began slapping him back and forth across the face. The man's head rocked to either side, sweat spraying from the few remaining clumps of hair on his pate. Fangatooth then kicked his brother's left shin, and then his right. Suddenly out of breath, he stepped back and swung round to Coingood. "Did you see that?"

"I did, milord."

"Write it down then! In detail!"

Coingood began scribbling again.

"And note my exultant pose, will you? This stance here, see how it exudes power? Somewhat wide-legged, as if I might jump in any direction. Arms held out but the hands hanging like . . . like the weapons of death that they are. Weapons of death, Scribe, you got that? Excellent. Now, look at me, I'm covered in blood. I need a change of clothes—wait, are you writing all that down? You damned fool. It was an aside, of course. That bit about my clothes. Tell me you've washed and dried my other black robe?"

"Of course, milord. Along with your other black vest, and your other black shirt and other black leggings."

"Excellent. Now, clean up around here. I will meet you in the Grand Chamber."

Coingood bowed. "Very well, milord."

After Fangatooth marched from the room, Coingood set down the tablet and studied it ruefully for a moment, noting how flecks of ash had marred the golden sheen of melted wax. "No wonder my eyes are going," he muttered.

"For the blessed gods of mercy, Coingood, release me!"

The scribe looked over at the wretched figure. "Them slaps weren't so bad, were they? The kicks to the shins, well, that must've smarted. But you have to agree, sir, today's session was a mild one."

"You're as evil as my brother!"

"Please, milord! I am in his service, and take my pay the same as the maids, cooks and all the rest! Does this make us all evil? Nonsense. What is evil, sir, is you inviting me to hardship and discomfort. I need to eat, don't I? Food on my table, a roof overhead and all that. Would you deny me such rights? In any case, how long would I survive defying your brother? Oh no, he wouldn't just fire me, would he? No, he'd *set* me on fire! Why, I'd be up in those chains, screaming myself hoarse. Do you really wish that on me, sir? All for a few moments of blessed freedom?"

Warmet's bleak eyes remained fixed on Coingood throughout the scribe's reasoned defense. Then he said, "My flesh is in ruin. My soul cries out in unending torment. The joints of my arms rage with fever. The muscles of my neck tremble with this effort to hold up my head. I was once a hale man, but look at me now, and wait to see me tomorrow, when I will be even worse. So, you will not lift a hand. Then I curse you, Coingood, as only a dying man can."

"That was cruel! Spiteful! I am not to blame! It is your brother who commands me!"

Warmet bared bloodstained teeth. "And there we are indeed different—you and me, Coingood. Look at me and know this: despite these chains, my soul remains free. But you . . . you have sold yours, and it came cheap."

There was a moan from the direction of the other man hanging in chains, and both Warmet and Coingood looked over that way, to see the prisoner stirring, drawing his legs under him and then slowly, agonizingly, standing to relieve the weight of his chains. His terribly scarred face swung to them, and the man said, "It's green and comes in all sizes, but that's all I'm giving you, Warmet."

Warmet's sweat-beaded brow wrinkled above the red weal of burnt flesh. "All right, give me a moment. Coingood's still here."

"Green—"

"I'm having a conversation, damn you!"

"You're down to four questions, Warmet!" the man sang.

"Shut up! I'm not ready to start again!"

"Four questions!"

"Bah! Solid or liquid?"

"Both! Hee hee!"

Coingood collected up his tablet and hurried from the chamber.

"Wait, Scribe! Where are you going?"

"I can't!" Coingood cried out. "Don't make me stay, milord!"

"You have gore, shit and piss to clean up—your master commanded it!"

Coingood halted almost within reach of the door's latch. "Unfair!" he whispered, pushing the scented cloth against his nose. But Warmet spoke the truth, damn him. He swung round. "Hot or cold?"

"You can't ask questions!" the other prisoner shrieked.

"Hot or cold?" Warmet shouted. "That's my next question!"

"In between!"

Sighing, Coingood said, "Snot."

"Cheaters!"

"Snot?" Warmet asked. "Is it snot? It's snot! Snot! I win!"

Feloovil Generous adjusted her breasts beneath the stained blouse and then sat down opposite the sailor with a heavy sigh. "We don't get many strangers visiting," she said, "for long."

The man shrugged, hands wrapped tight around the tankard of hot rum—a rather excessive amount of rum, but then he'd dropped a clean silver coin onto the table-top before she'd even finished pouring it, so she wasn't of a mind to advise him on medicinal portions—the man was chilled down to the marrow in his bones. She could see that. "Wreckers' lot," he said in a low, unsympathetic rumble.

"Well now," she replied, leaning back. "No reason to be unkind and all. Let's start anew. I'm Feloovil Generous, and I own the King's Heel."

"Happy for you," the sailor replied. "My name's Emancipor Reese. Not that you'll need to remember it, since we won't be here long. I hope."

"As long as you got the coin," she said, "you'll be welcome in here, is what I'm saying." She glanced over at Spilgit, who shared the table with the sailor, and scowled. "Take heed of that, Factor, since you got rent owing and the winter ahead's long and cold."

Spilgit leaned closer to Emancipor. "That's why she calls herself Generous, you see."

"Oh I'm generous enough," she retorted, "when it's appreciated. One thing I ain't generous about is some fool showing up calling himself a damned tax collector. We built this place up ourselves and we don't owe nobody nothing! Tell that to your prissy bosses, Spilgit!"

"I will, Feloovil, I will, and that's a promise!"

"You do just that!"

"I *will* do just that!"

"Go ahead, then!"

"I will!"

Ackle spoke from the window. "What's he doing with those bodies?"

Only Emancipor did not turn at that, still hunched over his steaming tankard and breathing deep the heady fumes.

Feloovil grunted her way upright and walked over to the inn's door. She pushed it open a crack. Then quickly drew her head back and swung to Spilgit. "That the one who killed the golem?"

"He was tearing out its insides when we come up," Spilgit said.

"How did he kill it?"

"No idea, Feloovil, but he did it and without getting a scratch!"

She realized she was having a conversation with the tax collector and quickly looked away, edging the door open a little further to watch Hordilo leading his two prisoners up the street towards Wurm Road. Spilgit showing up with her sweet daughter had been enough to make Feloovil want to slit the man's throat right then and there. But that kind of public murdering was bad for business, and more than a few of her girls would be pretty upset with her and that was never good. Instead, she'd sent Felittle up to her room to await a proper hiding. For the moment, that little slut-in-waiting could stew for a while longer.

Ackle edged up beside her and she recoiled slightly at his smell. "He's a bit too possessive for my liking," he then said, squinting up the street. "About those corpses, I mean."

She pulled him back inside and shut the door against the cold. "I told you, Risen, y'can sit at that one table since it's the smallest one here and out of the way of the others, and y'can keep my dogs happy, too, but you ain't a proper customer. So stop wandering around, will you? I swear I'll lock you out, Ackle, and leave you to freeze solid."

"Sorry, Generous." The man stumped back to his seat.

Thinking, Feloovil returned to Emancipor's table and sat down again across from him. "Spilgit, go away," she said. "Find another table, or go upstairs and say hi to the girls."

"You can't order—well, I suppose you can. All right, then, upstairs I go."

She waited until she heard his steps on the creaking stairs, and then leaned forward. "Listen, Emancipor Reese."

He'd drunk half the rum and when he looked up his eyes were bleary. "What?"

"Golems. They're sorcery, right? Powerful sorcery."

"I suppose."

"And Lord Fangatooth Claw's got three of 'em."

The man snorted. "Sorry, can't help it. Three, you said. Right. Two now, though."

"Exactly," she replied. "That's my point, right there."

He blinked at her. "Sorry? What was your point? I somehow missed it."

"Your masters—one of them went and killed one of those golems. That can't be easy, killing a heap of iron and whatnot."

"I wouldn't know," Emancipor said. "But take it from me, Korbal Broach has killed worse."

"Has he, now? That's interesting to hear. Very."

"But mostly it's Bauchelain you should be worried about," Emancipor went on, taking another deep mouthful of the rum.

"That the other one?"

"Aye. The other one."

"Sorcerers?"

The man nodded. And then laughed again. "Fangatooth!"

She shifted her considerable weight on the chair and
tried leaning even closer, but her breasts got in the way.
Cursing, she lifted one and thumped it down onto the
tabletop. Then did the same with the other. Glancing
up, she caught the look in Emancipor's eyes. "Aye, lovely,
ain't they? I'll introduce them to you later. Your masters, Emancipor Reese—"

"Mancy will do. Call me Mancy."

"Better, less of a Hood-damned mouthful anyway.
Mancy. They sorcerers?"

He nodded again.

"They're heading up to the keep, all on their own. Are
they stupid?"

Emancipor lifted one wavering finger. "Ah, now that's
an interesting question. I mean, there's all kinds of stupid,
izzn't there? Ever seen a ram butt its head against a rock?
Why a rock? Why, 'cause there's no other ram around,
thaz why. Your Fungletooth up there, been standing on
that rock all this time, right? All on his lonesome."

She studied him, and then slowly nodded. "Ever since
he imprisoned his brother, aye."

Emancipor waved carelessly. "Up there, then, maybe
they'll all butt heads—"

"And if they do? Who comes out on top?"

"—and maybe they don't."

"You're not getting it, Mancy. Butting heads sounds good. Butting heads sounds perfect. I like butting heads. You think it's fun living in fear?"

The man stared across at her, and then grinned. "Beats dying laughing, Floovle."

She rose. "Let's get some hearty food in you. So you can sober up. We got more talking to do, you and me."

"Do we?"

"Aye. Talking, and from talking we'll get to bargaining, and from bargaining we'll get to something else, something that'll make everyone happy. Sober up, Mancy. I got girls for you aplenty, and they're on the house."

"Kind of you," he replied, squinting up at her. "But girls just make me feel old."

"Better, cause then you got us."

"Us?"

She hefted her tits. "Us."

From a few paces away, Ackle flinched back when Feloovil proffered the sailor her breasts. "But then," he whispered, "if there's any good way to go . . ." He glanced across at the other patrons, regulars one and all, of course, and he supposed he was a regular now, too. Sort of. Funny how all the things he longed for in life just up and tumbled right into his lap now that he was dead.

But that was, in some ways, typical, wasn't it? Greatness was happiest with an ashen face, cloudy eyes and a demeanor unlikely to make any sudden unexpected moves. Even a mediocre man could climb into greatness by the simple act of dying. If he thought about history, these days, he saw in his mind's eye a whole row of great men and women, heroes and all that, and not one of them alive. No, instead they stood guard over great moments now long gone, and through it all stayed blind to whatever legacy their deeds left behind. It was selfish, in a way, but in a good way, too. Dying was a way to tell the world to just . . . *fuck off. Go fuck yourselves, you fucking fucks! Fuck off and fuck off forever and if you don't know what fucking forever is, take a look at us, you fuckers, we're fucking forever and we don't give a fuck about any of you, so just fuck . . . fuck . . . fuck off!*

He contemplated the possibility, in the wake of these thoughts, that he had some anger issues, which seemed pointless, all things considered. *It should hurt swallowing, shouldn't it? That rope didn't break my neck, well, maybe*

63

it did, who knows. Anyway, it was the choking that killed me. Suffocation, turning blue in the face, tongue poking out, eyes bulging. That kind of suffocation. So swallowing should hurt.

Fuck, do I want to kill them all? Hmm, difficult question. Let's mull on it some . . .

It's not like I've got anything else to do.

Still, that big, fat man, dragging those corpses. That's troubling all right. For a man like me, I mean. Dead, but not dead enough.

Between a rope and a pair of giant tits, I know which I'd rather suffocate from, and I doubt I'm alone in my learned opinion here. I doubt it sincerely. Ask any man. Ask any woman, too, for that matter. We're all heroes, so why not go out like one?

I should be standing in that line, back there in history, with a big fucking smile on my fucking face. But it doesn't hurt to swallow. Why is that?

Fuck!

Red, the lizard cat, bewildered once again by vague, troubling memories of walking on two feet and wearing clothes, stared at the two figures sitting side by side on the bed. He owned one of them, the one with the soft belly and the soft things above it that he liked to lie across when she slept. The other one, with his hands that slithered and his smells of lust wafting from him in pungent, whisker-twitching clouds, he didn't like at all.

Among his memories was the even stranger notion that once, long ago, there were more of him. He'd been dangerous back then, capable of ganging up on and then dragging down and killing men who bellowed and then shrieked and screamed that they wanted their eyes back, until jaws closed around the poor fool's throat and ripped and tore until it was all bloody and in shreds, with air bubbles frothing out and spurts that came in quick succession only to slow down, and finally fade into trickles. That was when he would feed, every one of him growing fat and torpid and eyeing places to lie up for a day or two.

Red wanted to kill the man on the bed.

What made things all the more infuriating, the lizard cat understood everything these two-legged creatures said, but his own fang-filled mouth ever failed to speak, and from his throat came nothing but incomprehensible purrs, hisses, moans and wavering wails.

Lying atop the dresser, Red was silent for the moment, eyes unblinking and fixed on the man's throat. Every now and then his thin, scaled tail twitched and curled.

The pink-throated man with the slithering hands was speaking. ". . . not thinking clearly, that's for sure. Hah hah! But there's no telling how long it'll last, Felittle."

"You can always hear her on the stairs, silly. Besides, we're not doing nothing, are we?"

"I shouldn't be in here. She's forbidden it."

"When I live in Elin, in that city, where you're taking me, there won't be nobody to tell me I can't have men in my room. So I will! Lots and lots of men, you'll see."

"Well, of course you will, darling," the man replied, with a tight smile that made Red's scales crackle down the length of his serrated back. "But then, you know, you might not want that."

"What do you mean?"

"One man might be enough for you, is what I'm saying, my love."

Felittle was blinking rapidly, her carmine lips parted in the way that always made Red want to slide his head between them, to look into the cavern of her mouth. Of course, his head was too big for that, but still, he longed to try. "One man? But . . . no woman wants just one man! No matter how much he pays! Where's the . . . the . . . variety? One man!" She yelped a laugh at her companion and punched him on the shoulder.

Such gestures were appallingly useless, with the nails

folded in like that. Far better, Red knew, if those short claws lashed out, slicing that shoulder to ribbons. There was no doubt in the lizard cat's mind that she needed proper protection, the kind of protection that Red could give. He rose slowly, affecting indifference, and lazily stretched out his back.

But the man noticed and his eyes narrowed. "Your damned cat's getting ready again. I swear, Felittle, when we go it's not coming with us. If it attacks me again, I'll punch it again, hard as I can."

"Oh, you're cruel!" cried Felittle, jumping from the bed and hurrying over to take Red into her arms. Over her shoulder, the lizard cat met the man's eyes and something passed between them that both instinctively understood.

By the time the flying scales and bits of flesh settled, one of them would stand triumphant. One of them, and only one, would possess this soft creature with the wide eyes. Red snuggled tighter and stretched open his mouth in a yawn, showing his rival his fangs. *See them, man-named-Slipgit?*

The display stole all colour from the man's face and he quickly looked away.

She snuggled Red closer. "My baby, ooh, my baby, it's all right. I won't let the big man hurt you again. I promise."

"It can't come with us," the man said.

"Of course he will!"

"Then you'd better forget about having lots of men in your room, Felittle. Unless you want them all sliced up and enraged and liable to take it out on the both of you."

Cooing, she slipped her hand to the back of Red's round head and held him so that she could peer into his face, only whiskers apart. "You'll get used to them, won't you, sweetie?"

Used to them? Yes. Used to killing them. Bellows, shrieks, screams about the eyes and then gurgles. But this elaborate and detailed answer came out as a low purr and a snuffle. Red exposed his claws and batted one paw in the man's direction.

At that he grunted and stood. "The problem with lizard cats," he said, "is that they kill the furry kind. Angry neighbours are never good, Felittle. In Elin, why, someone will strangle this thing before the first week's out."

"Oh, you're horrible! Not my Red!"

"If you want him to live for, er, however many years lizard cats live, you should leave him here. That's the best way of showing your love for Red."

No, the best way is tying you up and leaving you on the floor while she goes down for supper. I don't need long.

"Then maybe I won't go! Oh, Red, I so love your purring."

"You don't mean that."

"Oh, I don't know anymore! I'm confused!"

During this, Red had been gathering his limbs under him, moving slowly up onto her shoulder. Without warning, he launched himself at the man's face.

A fist collided with Red's nose, and then he was flying sideways, into the wall. Stunned, he fell to the floor beside the dresser. Something buzzed in his skull and he tasted blood. As if from a great distance, Red heard the man say, "You know, if that thing had any brains to speak of, it would try something different for a change."

Red felt hands slip under him and then he was lifted into the air, back into her arms. "Oh, you poor thing! Was Slippy mean to you again? Oh, he's so mean, isn't he?"

Something different? Now there's an idea. I need to remember this. I need to . . . oh, she's so soft, isn't she? Soft here, and soft here, too, and . . .

Whuffine Gaggs hummed under his breath as he pulled the silver ring from the severed finger and then tossed the finger into the spume-laden surf. It rolled back onto the sands with the next wave, as if trying to make a point, and then joined the others, jostling like sausages in a mostly even row above the fringe. A brief glance at them made his stomach rumble. Sighing, he squinted at the ring, which was thin but bore runic sigils running all the way round its surface. He saw the mark of the Elder God of the Seas, Mael, but little good that prayer had done the poor fool. Glancing down at the now-naked corpse at his feet, he studied her fleshy form for a moment longer, before shaking himself and with a muttered curse turned away.

A sharp grating sound made him look up to see a battered boat grounding prow-first against the wrack twenty paces up the beach. It looked abandoned, its oar-locks empty and the gunnels mostly chewed away, as if subject to frenzied jaws. Waves thumped into its stern, foamed over its square splashboard.

Grunting, Whuffine made his way over. As he drew near, cavalry boots crunching smartly in the sand with the jab of the walking stick making sweet punching sounds, he saw a man's head rise into view, and then a bandaged hand lifted in a frail wave. The face was deathly pale, except where a burn had taken away half the beard. Rimed in salt, the man could have crawled out from a pickling barrel.

"Ho there!" cried Whuffine, quickly pocketing the ring as he hurried closer. "Another survivor, thank Mael!" His free hand slipped beneath the sheepskins and deftly palmed the knife.

Red-rimmed eyes fixed on him, and then the man straightened. A short sword was belted to his waist, and he now settled a hand on it. "Back off, wrecker!" he said in a snarl, using the sea-trader's cant. "I ain't in the mood!"

Whuffine halted. "You look done in, sir! That's my shack up on the trail. Nice and warm, and I have food and drink."

"Do you now?" The man suddenly smiled, but it wasn't a pleasant smile. He looked down and seemed to nudge something with one foot. "Up, my love, we found us a friend."

A dark-skinned, mostly naked woman rose into view. Her left breast, brazenly exposed to the chill wintry air, was white as snow, but this absence of hue was uneven, its edges like splashes of paint. The look she settled upon Whuffine was full of suspicion. Moments later a third figure stirred upright in the boat. Blood-stained bandages covered most of his face, leaving only one eye clear, along with the lower jaw. "Thath's a wrecker all right," this man said, pausing to split and then lick his lips with a forked tongue. "I bet thath thack of hith ith a damned gallery of murder and worth, and crowded with loot bethideth."

"Just my point, Gust," said the first man. "We could do with some new gear, and stuff to sell, too." He then clambered over the side and stood on the sand. "Brisk, ain't it?" he asked Whuffine. "But it ain't no Stratem winter, is it?" He then drew his sword. "Put the knife away, fool, and lead us up to the shack."

Whuffine eyed the weapon, noting the savage nicks along both edges. "I'm not going to take kindly to being robbed, and since the only town for leagues in any direction is just up the trail, where I have lots of friends, and where the Lord of the Keep is stickler about law and order, you'd be making a terrible mistake doing me harm, or cleaning me out."

The one-eyed man loosed a laugh verging on hysteria. "Lithen to him, Heck, he'th threatening uth! Hah hah hah! Ooh, I'm thcared! Hah hah!"

"Stop that, Gust," snapped the woman. "The point is, we gotta get going. Those Chanters ain't all dead, you know, and I bet they'll want their lifeboat back—"

"Too late!" shrieked the man named Gust.

"They went down, Birds," said Heck. "They must've! There was fire and screamin' dead men and demons and Korbal Broach and the sharks—gods the sharks! All with

Mael's own storm crashing down on us! Nobody survived that!"

"We did," Birds reminded him.

Heck licked his lips, and then shook himself. "It don't matter, love." He rubbed at his face, wincing when his fingers touched the weal of the burn. "Let's go and get warm. We can plan over a meal and a keg of ale. The point is, we're on dry land again, and I don't mean to ever go back to sea. You, wrecker, where in Hood's name are we?"

"Elingarth," Whuffine replied.

"Nothing but pirates," hissed Birds, "the whole lot of them. Who's up in that keep, then? Slormo the Sly? Kabber the Slaughterer? Blue Grin the Wifestealer?"

Whuffine shook his head. "Never heard of those," he said.

"Of courth you didn't," said Gust. "They all been dead a hundred yearth! Birdth, thothe thailor taleth were old when you were thtill farming clamth with your Da." He waved a bandaged hand. "We don't care who'th up at the keep, anyway. It'th not like we're getting an invite to dine, ith it? With the lord, I mean."

"Oh," said Whuffine, brightening, "I expect the lord will indeed invite you into his keep. In fact, I'm sure of it. Why, he's already entertaining your companions—"

"Our what?" Birds asked.

"Why, the elderly nobleman with the pointy beard, and his manservant—" He stopped then as Heck was clambering back into the boat.

"Push us off!" he screamed.

"Excuse me?"

But all three were scrabbling back and forth in the boat, as if by panic alone they could make the craft move.

"Push us off!" shrieked Heck.

Whuffine shrugged, walked over to the prow and set his shoulder against it. "I don't understand," he said between grunts. "You've been saved, spared by the storm, good people. Why risk another, and you so unprepared for any sort of sea voyage—"

The tip of Heck's shortsword pressed up against Whuffine's neck, and the man leaned close. "Listen to me if you value your life! Get us off this cursed beach!"

Whuffine gaped, swallowed delicately, and then said, "You'll all have to climb out and help, I'm afraid. You're too heavy. But I beg you all, don't do this! You'll die out there!"

The bandaged man laughed again, this time in the jabbering grip of hysteria. The other two scrambled from the boat and began tugging and pulling and pushing, feet digging deep furrows in the wet sand. Whuffine resumed his efforts and together they managed to dislodge the craft. Heck and Birds leapt back in and Whuffine, wincing at what the salt water would do to his boots, edged out into the waves and gave the boat a final shove. "But you have no oars!"

Hands paddled furiously.

The surf battled against their efforts, but after some time the boat was clear of the worst of the swells, and at last making headway out to sea.

Whuffine stared after them for a time, confused and more than a little alarmed. Then he returned to the corpses on the strand, and cutting off fingers and whatnot.

The sea was a strange realm, and the things it offered up on occasion passed comprehension, no matter how wise the witness. There was no point, Whuffine knew, in questioning such things. Ugly as fate, the world did what it did and never asked permission either.

He moved to the next body and began stripping the clothes away, eyes darting in search of jewelry, coin-pouches or anything else of value. Like his father used to say, the sea was like a drunk's mouth: there was no telling what might come out of it. Or go back in.

. . .

Hordilo Stinq made a fist and pounded on the thick wooden door. He was slightly out of breath from the climb, but the effort had warmed him up some. As they waited, alas, he could feel the cold seeping back in. "Normally it's not a long wait," he said. "Lord Fangatooth has sleepless servants, ever watching from those dark slits up there."

The man named Bauchelain was studying the massive wall rearing up to either side of the gatehouse. The remnants of a few corpses still remained, hanging from the hooks they had been impaled on. The heads, still bearing tufts of weathered hair and a few sections of dried skin, were all tilted at unnatural angles and the effect, from directly below where stood Hordilo, was that of being looked down upon, with toothy smiles and empty eye sockets. At the foot of the wall more bones were jumbled in disordered heaps.

"This keep is very old indeed," Bauchelain then said. "It reminds me of the one I was born in, to be honest, and I find this curious detail most enticing." He turned to his companion. "What think you, Korbal my friend? Shall we abide here for a time?"

But Korbal Broach was stripping down the two corpses he'd dragged all the way from the beach, flinging the sodden, half-frozen garments aside and prodding exposed, pallid flesh with a thick finger. "Will they keep, Bauche-lain?" he asked.

"In this cold, I should imagine so."

"I will leave them here for now," Korbal replied, straightening. He walked up to the heavy door and closed his hand on the latch.

"It's locked, of course," said Hordilo. "We must await the lord's pleasure."

But the huge man twisted until the iron bent, and then there was a muted snapping sound from the door's other side, followed by something striking the floor. Korbal Broach pushed the door open and strode inside.

Appalled, Hordilo rushed after the man. They crossed the broad, shallow cloakroom and emerged into the main hall before Hordilo was able to interpose himself in the man's path. "Have you lost your mind?" he demanded in a hoarse whisper.

Korbal Broach swung round to Bauchelain. "He is in my way," he said. "Why is he in my way?"

"I would expect," Bauchelain replied, stepping past and adjusting his cloak momentarily, "that this consta-ble serves his lord from a place of bone-deep fear. Terror, even. I for one find the relationship between a master and his or her minions to be ever problematical. Terror, after all, stultifies the higher processes of the intellect.

Independent judgment suffers. As a consequence, our escort finds his position most awkward, and now fears his potential demise as a result."

"I have decided that I don't like him, Bauchelain."

"I am reminded of Mister Reese, on his first day in our employ, as he stood belligerent against an intruder in defense of our privacy. See this man before you, Korbal, as a victim of panic. Of course you may kill him if you wish, but then, who would make introductions?"

Heavy footsteps were drawing nearer, each plod rumbling like thunder through the stone tiles of the floor.

"A golem approaches!" gasped Hordilo. "Now you've done it!"

"Do step aside, sir," Bauchelain advised. "It may be that we are forced to defend ourselves."

Eyes wide, Hordilo backed to the wall beside the entranceway. "This has nothing to do with me! Not anymore!"

"Wise decision, sir," murmured Bauchelain, sweeping clear his cloak to reveal a heavy black chain surcoat and a longsword strapped to his belt, the bone handle vanishing inside a gauntleted grasp as the man readied to draw free the weapon.

His companion now faced towards the sound of the approaching footsteps.

They were all startled by a voice from the other side

of the chamber. "Hordilo! What in Hood's name is going on? Go close that damned door! It's chilly enough in here without the added draft!"

"Scribe Coingood!" Hordilo gasped in relief. "I arrested these men—that one there killed Grimled! And then he broke the lock on the door and then he—"

"Be quiet!" Coingood snapped, setting down the bucket he carried and then leaning his mop against a wall. Brushing his hands, he strode forward. "Guests, is it?"

"They killed Grimled!"

"So you say, Hordilo, so you say. How unfortunate."

"I would certainly describe it in just that manner," Bauchelain said. "And I trust, good sir, that your master will not hold it against us."

"Well, as it took him five months to animate the thing, I expect he'll be somewhat upset," Coingood replied.

At that moment the golem arrived. By the rust rimming its pail-shaped head Hordilo knew it to be Gorebelly. Hinges squealing, the abomination thumped to a halt and slowly raised its halberd.

Impossibly, Korbal Broach was suddenly standing in front of it, plucking the heavy weapon effortlessly from the golem's iron hands and flinging it aside. He then reached up and twisted off Gorebelly's head. Fluids gushed from the gaping throat. The headless apparition staggered back a step, and then toppled. Its impact on the floor shattered tiles.

Still clutching the dripping iron bucket, Korbal turned to face them, a deep frown lining his brow. "It broke," he said.

"See!" Hordilo shrieked, rushing towards Coingood. "That's what he does!"

The scribe was very pale. Licking dry lips, he cleared his throat and said, "Ah, well. I had best summon my master, I think."

"Sound judgment," said Bauchelain.

"I'll go with you!" Hordilo said.

"No. Stay here, Sergeant. I won't be but a moment, I assure you."

"You can't leave me with them!"

Sighing, Coingood turned to Bauchelain. "I trust you can constrain your companion, sir, and so assure the sergeant here that no one will tear off his head or anything."

"Ah, we are ever eager for assurances, it's true," Bauchelain replied. "Only to invariably discover that the world cares nothing for such things. That said, I am confident that the sergeant will get to keep his head for a while longer."

Hordilo stepped close to Coingood. "Please, don't leave me alone with them!"

"We'll be right back. Show some courage here, damn you!"

Hordilo watched the scribe hurry off. Although they were now inside the keep, still he shivered. Setting his back against a wall, he eyed the two men opposite. Korbal Broach had upended the golem's iron head and was shaking out the last few rattling bits left inside it. Bauchelain was removing his gauntlets one finger at a time.

"Dear sergeant," the tall man then said. "About your lord . . ."

Hordilo shook his head. "That won't work."

Brows rising, Bauchelain shrugged. "Simple curiosity on my part, nothing more."

"I've done my part and that's all I'm doing."

"Of course. But now . . . do you regret it?"

"The only one regretting anything will be you two. Lord Fangatooth Claw is also known as The Render, and it's a title well earned!"

"Surely it should be 'The Renderer'?"

"What?"

Sounds from the corridor drew their attention. Korbal Broach dropped the golem's iron head and the clang echoed shrilly in the chamber.

Moments later Coingood appeared and a step behind him was Lord Fangatooth.

Hordilo saw his master's eyes fix on the decapitated golem lying on the broken tiles. His expression revealed nothing.

"Korbal, my friend," said Bauchelain, "I believe you owe the lord an apology for your mishandling of his golems."

"Sorry," Korbal said, his flabby lips strangely stained by the fluids from the golem, as if he had but moments earlier licked his fingers.

"Yes, well," said Fangatooth. "Their sole purpose, of course, was to instill fear in the villagers. Now, as I understand it, but one remains. I see a busy winter ahead." He swept his black cloak back from his shoulders. "I am Lord Fangatooth Claw, Master of the Forgotten Holding, High Sorcerer of the Lost Gods of Ilfur, Seneschal of Grey Arts, High Mage of Elder Thelakan and last surviving member of the League of Eternal Allies." He paused, and then said, "I understand that you are survivors of an unfortunate shipwreck."

"We are," replied Bauchelain. "This is a fine keep, sir, in which every chill draught evokes nostalgia. As a child I once haunted an edifice quite similar to this one. This has the feel of a homecoming."

"I am pleased," Fangatooth replied with a tight smile. He then turned to Coingood. "Scribe, be sure the best rooms are prepared for our guests. Furthermore, you will attend our supper this evening with all the wax tablets at your disposal, for I anticipate a lively discourse."

"Our manservant," said Bauchelain, "is presently recovering from his ordeals at a tavern in the village."

"Sergeant Hordilo will collect him," Fangatooth said. "Although I assure you, my own staff can see to all of your needs."

"Of that I have no doubt, sir, but I am partial to Mister Reese."

"Understood. Now, by what titles are you two known?"

"Such titles as we may have accrued in our travels," said Bauchelain, "are both crass and often the product of misunderstanding. Our names should suffice. I am Bauchelain and my companion is Korbal Broach."

"Yet of noble blood, I presume?"

"Most noble, sir, most noble. But we have travelled far—"

"In the company of misfortune, it seems," cut in Fangatooth, finally showing his teeth in the smile he offered his guests.

Bauchelain waved one pale, long-fingered hand. "If the past pursues, it is leagues in our wake. While the future holds only promise, and should that promise be nothing more than one foot following the other, pray it continues without end."

Fangatooth frowned, and then he said, "Yes, just so. Please, my dear guests, shall we retire to the sitting room? A fire burns in the hearth and mulled wine awaits us, in keeping with the season. Scribe? I trust you have recorded this momentous . . . moment?"

"I have indeed, milord."

"Excellent!"

"I wonder, good sir," ventured Bauchelain, "if this keep has a spacious kitchen?"

"It has. Why do you ask?"

"As I said earlier. Nostalgia. It was in the kitchen where I skulked the most as a child, and where, indeed, I learned the art of baking."

"Baking? How curious."

"I would be delighted with a tour later."

"I don't see why not."

Bauchelain smiled.

"What wuz I drinking?" Emancipor asked, as the room tilted back and forth, as if he still stood on a deck, amidst rolling swells. The walls bowed in sickly rhythm, the floor lifting and falling beneath him.

"Rum," said Feloovil. "You're celebrating."

"I am? What's happened, then, for to be celerbating. Brating. Celeb . . . rating."

"The death of Lord Fangatooth Claw, of course."

"He's dead?"

"About to be."

"Is he sick, then?"

She scowled. "Listen, sober up, will you? You got half a pot of stew in you, damn me, and that wasn't for free neither."

"I'm sober enough. It's you who ain't making any sense."

"They're up there, right? In the keep. All together, the three of them. Blood will spill, and who will be left standing when it's all done? You told me—"

"Oh, that." Emancipor spread his legs wider to keep his balance. Feloovil swayed before him.

"They'll kill him, won't they?"

"Probbly."

She smiled. "That's what I like to hear, friend. Oh yes, and for that, why, it's time for your reward."

"It's my birthday," said Emancipor.

"It is?"

"Must be. Celerbating, rewards, but then, how do you know it's my birthday? I don't even know what day this is, or month for that matter." He shook his head. "You probbly got it wrong, which is typical, since everyone does. Or they forget. Like me. Is there any more rum? I'm not warmed up yet."

"Let me warm you up," Feloovil said, stepping closer. "Here, grab these. No, one for each hand. No, you keep missing. How can you miss these?"

"They won't sit still, that's why."

"I named them, you know."

"You did? Why?"

"Now that's my secret, only you're about to find out. Just you. Only you. It was a gift, you see. From Witch Hurl, who ruled here years back—"

"What happened to her?"

"No one knows. She just vanished one night. But that don't matter, Mancy. It's what she gave me. She had this statue, right? Very old. Some earth goddess or someone. She took all her power from it, for her magicks. In any case, whoever carved that statue could've been using me as a model, if you know what I mean."

"I thought you said it was old. How old are you, then?"

She scowled. "No, it wasn't me. But it could've been. Especially my friends here—no, don't look around, you idiot. The tits you're holding. This one here, her name's Stout, on account of her staying firm the way she does. And the other one's Sidelopp, on account of . . . well."

"You've named your tits?"

"Why not? They're my friends."

"As in . . . bosom companions?"

Her eyes thinned. "Oh," she said, "I never thought of that one before. Thanks. Now, let go of them so I can get this tunic off, so you can see what she did to them. To make them just like the statue's tits."

"I thought you said they already were."

"Almost, but now, aye, they are, Mancy."

He watched while she turned her back, as if suddenly succumbing to modesty, and shrugged and tugged her way out of the heavy, stained tunic. Then she turned around.

Her breasts had no nipples. Instead, in place of them, were mouths, with soft, feminine lips painted bright red. As he stared, both tits blew him a kiss.

"They got teeth, too," Feloovil said. "And tongues. But they can't talk, which is probably a good thing. I think it's a good thing, at least. Watch while I make them lick their lips."

Emancipor spun round, staggered to the nearest corner of the room and threw up.

"Hey!" Feloovil shouted behind him. "That was half a pot of my best stew, damn you!"

Spilgit leaned away from the wall. "She yelled something," he whispered. "And then started berating him. Something about thinking he was a man of the world, only he isn't. And then there were footsteps and someone trying to get out of the room."

"Only Ma's locked it," Felittle said. "He can't get out."

Spilgit frowned across at her. "She's done this before? What's she doing to him? She locks men in her room? Why do they want to get out? Well, I mean, I would, but then I'd never go into her room in the first place. But he did, so he knew what was coming, more or less, didn't he? But I swear I heard him gag, or something. It sounded like a gag—wait, is she strangling him or something? Does she kill them, Felittle? Is your mother a mass murderer?"

"How should I know?" she demanded from where she sat on the bed, her lizard cat sprawled across her thighs, the creature watching Spilgit with unblinking, yellow eyes. "Maybe I've seen her bury a body or two, out back. But that happens. It's an inn, after all, with people in beds and old men trying to die smiling, and all that."

"She's buried people out back?"

"Well, dead ones, of course. Not like Ackle."

"Ackle wasn't dead."

"Yes he was."

"Not a chance. The noose strangled him bad, that's true, and probably killed bits of his brain, which was why he looked dead to everyone. But he wasn't, and that's why he came back. Gods below, I can't believe the superstitions you have here in this wretched backwater. No, you've not treated him well since then, have you? It's a disgrace."

Felittle blinked at him. "Backwater? Are you calling Spendrugle, where I was born, a backwater? So what am I, then? A backwaterian? Is that what I am to you, Mister Big Smelly City?"

Spilgit hurried over, recoiling at the last moment from Red's savage hiss and raised hackles. "Darling, of course not. Every dung heap has a hidden gem, and you're it. I mean, if I didn't find you lovely and all, would I offer to help you escape? And," he went on, still trying to get closer but Red was now on its feet, dorsal spines arching and ears flattened and mouth opened wide, "if you didn't think this was a backwater you wouldn't want to get away, would you?"

"Who says I want to get away?"

"You do! Don't you remember, my sweet?"

"It was you who wanted to steal me away, and I listened and all, and so you convinced me. But maybe I like it here, and once Ma lets me start working with the other girls, I'll—"

"But she won't, Felittle," Spilgit said, looking for something he could use as a weapon on the cat. "That's just it. She'll never let you do that. She'll see you stay a virgin, a spinster, all your life. You know it, too." He found a brass candlestick on the dresser and collected it up.

"But then you said you weren't going to let me have lots of men in the city, so what's the point of me going with you anywhere? You'll end up just like Ma, chaining me in some cellar! What are you doing with that?"

He advanced on her, hefting the candlestick. "Is that how you really want it? You want me to hire you out for the night, to whoever's got the coin?"

"Oh, will you? Yes, please! What are you doing with that candlestick?" she backed up on the bed. "How many bodies have you buried behind the tax office, that's what I'm wondering now!"

"Don't be silly. Tax collectors want people to live forever, of course. Getting older and older, so we can strip from them every single hard-won coin."

"Put that thing down!"

"Oh, I'll put something down all right. Count on it."
He raised the candlestick.

Red leapt at his face.

He swung with all his strength.

Emancipor Reese clawed fruitlessly at the lock on the
door. Behind him, Feloovil laughed a deep, throaty laugh.
"It's no use, Mancy, we've got you for the night, and when
I say we're going to cover your body in kisses, I do mean
it, don't I? Kisses and bites and nips and—"

"Open this damned door!" Emancipor snarled, spinning round and reaching for his sword.

But Feloovil had raised one hand. "Shh! Listen! I hear
voices in my daughter's room! Voices! Gods below, it's
Spilgit!" She collected up her tunic from the floor and
began pulling it on. "That's it, he's a dead man for this.
And I'm calling in his tab, too. Can't pay, can't leave, ever.
Can't pay, it's the backyard for you!"

Edging away from the door as Feloovil produced a key
from somewhere beneath her tunic, Emancipor drew
his shortsword. "Good, open it, aye. Before things get ugly
here."

"Ugly?" She barked a laugh. "You're about to see ugly,

Mancy, like no ugly you've ever seen in that miserable, sheltered existence you call a life." She unlocked the door.

They were startled by a loud thump on the wall, followed by broken plaster striking the floor beside Feloovil's bed.

Something had come through the wall, halfway to the ceiling. As the dust cloud cleared, Emancipor saw a lizard cat's head, its nose draining blood, its eyes blinking but not synchronously. It seemed to be winking at them.

With Feloovil standing motionless, staring at the cat's head, Emancipor made his move, pushing hard to get past her and into the corridor. Without a look back, he rushed for the stairs. Behind him he heard Feloovil bellow, and someone else was now screaming. Reaching the stairs, Emancipor plunged downward—and coming fast behind him was another set of footsteps. Growling a curse, Emancipor looked back over one shoulder. But it was Spilgit who was on his way down, with Feloovil thundering after him.

Reaching the ground floor, Emancipor ran down the length of the bar to the door.

It opened then, revealing Hordilo, who pointed a finger at Emancipor and said, "You!"

. . .

Despite the bitter cold, the half-frozen sand Whuffine turned over with his shovel stank of urine. He'd already excavated a decent hole, and had begun to wonder if his memory had failed him, when his shovel struck something hard. Redoubling his efforts, he quickly worked the object loose, and lifted into view a pitted and suitably stained stone idol. Grunting, he heaved it out of the pit and set it down on the sand for a closer look.

It had been a few years since he'd buried the thing beneath his piss trench, but the chisel work now looked centuries old. Come the spring, after the winter's hard weathering, he could load it onto his cart and take it into the village. If anything, this one was better than the last effort, and hadn't Witch Hurl paid a bagful of silver coins for that one? For all he knew, Fangatooth might be just as happy to kneel in worship before an idol from the Ancient Times.

The creation of true art had a way of serendipity, and if he hadn't snapped off a nipple on the final touches with the last one, he'd never have found the need to re-work it into a mouth instead, and then do the same to the other nipple, inventing a whole new goddess of earth, sex, milk and whatever. This time, he had elaborated on the theme, adding a third mouth, down below.

Hearing more voices from the beach, he climbed out of the stinking pit and brushed gritty sand from his hands.

The boat was back, and this time the three sailors were piling out to scrabble their way up towards the trail, the bandaged one limping and already falling behind the others.

Collecting his shovel, Whuffine awaited them.

"Come to your senses, did you? No wonder. There's another blow coming in . . ."

But the three simply swept past, gasping, moaning and whimpering as they hurried up the trail. Whuffine stared after them, frowning. "I've got warm broth!" he shouted, to no effect. Shrugging, he set down the shovel again and collected up the idol. He'd walk it down to the water, off to the left of the sands where the rocks made ragged spines reaching out into the bay. Lodged amidst those rocks, the idol would sit, gnawed by salt and cold and hard waves day and night for the next few months.

Whuffine was halfway to the spines when he saw the other boat, coming in fast.

. . .

Gasping in pain, Spilgit limped up the street. If Feloovil hadn't stumbled at the last moment, that knife would have found his back instead of his right calf. Shivering with shock, he approached his office. It took a strange person to decide to become a tax collector, and over the past month he had come to the conclusion that maybe he wasn't cut out for it.

He thought back to his days in Elin, when he was first apprenticed to the trade. Taxation in a city ruled by pirates was a bold notion, to be sure, and its practice was a vicious affair. They'd all trained in weapons and the detection of poison, and a few of his fellow apprentices had indeed plunged into the grey arts. On one day each year, the day that taxes were due, not even the Enclave bodyguards attached to each and every collector could be trusted. Spilgit's final year in the city had seen almost sixty percent losses in the Guild, and more than one chest of tax revenue disappeared in the chaos.

He'd thought this distant posting would be a welcome escape from the horrors of Elin's Day of Blood and Taxes. He'd displayed few of the necessary talents to imagine a long and prosperous life in Elin as a tax collector. He wasn't coldhearted enough. He lacked the essential knot of cruelty in his soul, the small-minded descent into arbitrary necessities upon which collectors founded their arguments justifying blatant theft and the bullying and threats essential to successful extortion. Instead, he had revealed a soft ear for sob stories, for terrible tragedies and sudden house fires and mysterious burglaries and missing coin. He wept for the limping man tottering on his stick, for the snotty runts clinging to a destitute mother smelling of wine and sour milk, for the wealthy landowner swearing that he had not a single coin in his purse.

The worst of it was, he had actually believed that the taxes he collected went to answering worthy needs, and all the necessities of governance and the maintenance of law and order, when in truth most of it filled the war-chests of gouty nobles whose only talent was hoarding.

No, this journey into the empty wastelands out here in the realm's dubious borderlands had taught him much, about himself, and about the world in general. Feloovil's attempted murder would go unpunished. She offered too essential a service in Spendrugle. He, Spilgit, was the unwanted man.

Pushing open the door to his office, he staggered inside and made his way to the lone chair. The woodstove still emanated remnants of heat and he fed more scraps of driftwood onto the coals. *But that was all before today. I'm not the same man I used to be. I'm not soft anymore. I am now capable of murder, and when I return to Elin, with that idiotic lovely cow in tow, why, I will sell her and feel not a single qualm, since she'll be blissfully happy.*

And I will be a tax collector. With iron for eyes, a mouth thinned to a dagger's edge, straight and disinclined to warp into anything resembling a genuine smile. No, this up-turn of this here mouth, it signals the delightful pleasure of evil.

Evil: the way it flows out from the deed, the way it spreads its stain of injustice. Evil: smelling of sweet lies and bitter truths. We own the tax laws. We know every way around them, meaning we never pay up a single sliver of tin, but you do, oh yes, you do.

He struggled to wrap a cloth around his wounded calf, cursing his numbed fingers. At least, he consoled him-self, he had killed the cat. There was no way it could have survived, despite its twitching body, or the way it sank its claws into the wall, spread-eagled as it tried to pull its head free, tail curling like a wood shaving to the flicker of flame. Oh, who was he kidding? The damned thing still lived.

And if the roads fall into ruin, and the city guards starve without their bribes; and people live on the streets and need to sell their children to make ends meet. And if the judges are all bought off and the jailers sport gold rings, and everything that was once free now costs, why, that's just how it is, and which side of the wall do I want to be standing on?

He understood things now. He saw with utter clarity. The world was falling into ruin, but then it was always falling into ruin. Once that was comprehended, why, the evil of every moment—this entire endless realm of *now*—made perfect sense. He would join the others, all those bloated greed merchants, and ride the venal present, and to Hood with the future, and to Hood with the past. The Lord of Death awaited them all in the end anyway.

The door scraped open and Spilgit bleated, reaching for his knife.

"It's just me," said Ackle, peering in.

"Gods below!"

"Can I join you? I brought some wood."

Spilgit waved him in. "Try and close that behind you. Funny you should drop by, Ackle. It occurs to me that we have something in common."

"Aye, we're both dead men."

Spilgit sighed, and then rubbed at his face. "If we stay in Spendrugle all winter, we are."

"Well, I could stay around. Unless I freeze solid. Then Hordilo will burn me in a pyre and I saw the look in his eyes when he said that. It's all down to Feloovil being nice to me, and that's why I'm here, in fact."

"What do you mean?"

"I mean, all is forgiven. And if that's not enough, why, Feloovil has decided to wipe clean your tab. And you still have your room."

Spilgit studied the man levelly. "You should be ashamed of yourself, Ackle."

"The dead are beyond shame, Spilgit. That said, I admit to some qualms, but like I said, I need somewhere warm for the winter."

"She actually expects me to go back to the Heel with you? Arm in arm?"

"Well, it's hard to say, honestly. She is a bit beside herself at the moment. Poor Felittle is distraught, with what you did to her."

"I didn't do anything to her! The cat attacked me and I defended myself."

"Then it went and attacked Feloovil, too, once it got its head out of the wall. And then the damned thing attacked just about everybody else—all the customers and half the girls, and down in the bar, well, it was chaos. The place is a shambles. Two dead dogs, too, their throats ripped out. I take that bit hard, by the way."

Slipgit licked his lips, and then pointed a finger at

Ackle. "Didn't I warn them? Didn't I? Lizard cats can't be domesticated! They're vicious, treacherous, foul-tempered and they smell like moulted snakeskin."

"I wasn't aware of any smell," Ackle said.

"Did they kill it?"

"No, it got away, but Feloovil swore she'd skewer it if it ever tried to come back, which made Felittle burst into tears again, and that got all the girls going, especially when the customers started demanding their money back, or at least compensation for wounded members and such."

"What was Hordilo doing during all of this?"

"Gone, escorting that manservant up to the keep. He said he'd never seen such a scene since his wife left. Not that he was ever married."

"Before my time," Spilgit muttered, shrugging and looking out the small window, peering through patches in the ice. "Anyway, if I go back with you, she'll kill me."

"At least it'll improve her mood."

"And this is proof of how people just look out for themselves! Which is precisely why they all hate tax collectors. It's the one time when someone is asking something of you, from you, and you get that murderous look in your eye and start blathering on about theft and extortion and corruption and all the rest. Take any man or woman and squeeze them and they start making the same sounds, the same whimpers and whines, the same wheedling and moaning. They'd rather bleed themselves than give up a coin!"

"I'm sorry, Spilgit, but what's your point? In any case, it's not like you can tax me, is it? I'm dead."

"You're not dead!"

"Just what a tax collector would say, isn't it?"

"You think we don't know that scam? Faking your death to avoid paying? You think we're all idiots?"

"I'm not faking anything. I was hanged. You saw it yourself. Hanged until dead. Now I'm back, maybe to haunt you."

"Me?"

"How many curses do you imagine are hanging over you, Spilgit? How many demons are waiting for you once you die? How many fiery realms and vats of acid? The torment you deliver in this mortal life will be returned upon you a thousandfold, the day you step through Hood's gate."

"Rubbish. We sell you that shit so we can get away with whatever we damn well please. 'Oh, I'll get mine in the end!' Utter cat-turd, Ackle. Who do you think invented religion? Tax collectors!"

"I thought religion was invented by the arbitrary

hierarchy obsessed with control and power to justify their elite eminence over their enslaved subjects."

"Same people, Ackle."

"I don't see you lording it over any of us here, Spilgit."

"Because you refuse to accept my authority! And for that I blame Lord Fangatooth Claw!"

"Feloovil says that the manservant's masters are going to kill him."

Spilgit leaned forward. "Really? Give me that wood, damn you. Let's get some heat in here. Tell me more!"

With Sordid and Bisk Fatter working the oars, Wormlick was up at the prow, studying the beach ahead with narrowed eyes. "He's a comber, I'd say," he said in a hoarse growl. "No trouble to us, and that's their boat, pulled up on the strand."

There'd be words. There'd be answers, even if Wormlick had to slice open their bellies and pull out their intestines. Most of all, there'd be payback. He scratched vigorously through his heavy beard, probed with light fingertips the small red rings marking his cheeks. He'd have to cut them out again, never a pleasant task, and he never got them all out. The damned worms knew when they were under assault, and spat eggs out in panic, and before too long he'd have more rings on his face, and neck. It was all part of his life, like cutting his hair, or washing out his underclothes. Once a month, every month, for as long as he could remember.

But getting back the loot stolen from them, why, he could find a proper healer. A Denul healer, who would take his coin and rid him of the worms that had given him his name. Coin could pay for anything, even a return to beauty, and one day, he'd be beautiful again.

"Almost there!" he called back over his shoulder. The comber had carried a big rock down to one side of the crescent beach, where he'd left it lodged right where the waves thrashed the shore. Now he had walked back to await them, his sheep-skin cloak flapping about in the wind. "He's old, this one. Was a big man once, probably trouble, but that was decades past. Still, let's keep an eye on him. We're too close to see it all go awry now."

They had pursued the *Suncurl* since Toll's Landing. Left to drown only a rope's throw from the ship, they had seen their comrades, Birds Mottle, Gust Hubb and Heck Urse, looking back on them from the rail, doing nothing, just standing there watching them drown.

But we didn't drown, did we? No, we don't drown easily.

*We stole the Chanter's hoard together, with Sater running
the plan, only to be betrayed, and now we want our take,
and damn me, but we're going to get it.*

Glancing to his left, he studied the wreckage of the
Suncurl. He and his companions weren't the only ones
chasing that doomed, cursed ship. There'd been a clash
with the Chanters, but the storm had broken them apart
and if the gods were smiling, those Chanters had all
gone down to the black world of mud and bones, a
thousand fathoms below. In any case, they'd seen no
sign of the wretched bastards since the first night of the
storm.

The longboat ground heavily into the sand, jolting
them all.

Sordid rose, sweeping back her flaxen hair, and arched
her back before turning round and eyeing the comber.
She snorted. "Nice hat. I want that hat."

"Later," Bisk Fatter said, pitching himself over the side
and wading ashore.

Wormlick followed.

Walking towards the comber, Bisk drew out his two-
handed sword.

The man backed up. "Please, I've done nothing!"

"This is simple," Bisk said. "So simple you might even
live. Heck Urse. Birds Mottle. Gust Hubb. Where are
they?"

"Ah." The comber gestured to where a trail was cut into the sloped bank above the beach, near a shack. "Off to the village, I would think. Spendrugle, upon the mouth of the Blear and beneath Wurms Keep. It is likely they are warming themselves at the King's Heel, on the High Street."

Bisk sheathed his sword and turned to Wormlick and Sordid. "We're back on land," he said, "and I'm corporal again. I give the orders, understood?"

Wormlick eyed his companion. Bisk was barely the height of his sword, but he had the build of a rock-ape, and a face to match. Those small eyes so deep in their shadowy, ringed sockets were like the blunted fingernails of a corpse from a man who'd been buried alive in a coffin. When he smiled, which was mercifully infrequent, he revealed thick pointy teeth, stained blue by urlit leaves. In his life he had killed thirty-one men, seven women and one child who'd spat on his boot and then laughed and said, "You can't touch me! It's the law!"

Bisk was a man pushed into military service, but then, so were they all, in the days when Toll and most of Stratem were waiting for the invasion. But the Crimson Guard landed only to leave again; and then the Chanters decided to take over everything, and life turned sour.

All behind them now.

"All right, sir," Sordid said with a shrug, standing loose the way she did when she was thinking of stabbing someone in the back. It was a miracle they'd not killed each other, but the deal was a sure one. Get back the loot, and then the blades could clash. But not until then.

"Let's go," said Bisk. He pointed at the comber. "Good answers. You live."

"Thank you, good people! Bless you!"

The three ex-guards of Toll's City made for the trail.

Whuffine Gaggs watched the three walk past his shack, leaving it undisturbed. At that, the comber sighed. "That could have been trouble, that's for sure." He eyed the fine longboat rocking on the beach, and went to collect up its bowline. The big blow was coming back, like a whore finding a wooden coin, and he wanted to batten things down and be sitting warm and cozy in his shack by the time the furies arrived. This boat was worth a lot, after all, and he wasn't expecting to see those three fools again.

But the boat wasn't the only task awaiting him. Indeed, he had plenty to do before nightfall.

Whistling under his breath, he tied the bow rope around his chest, looped his right arm under it and then leaned forward. A boat built for twelve was a heavy beast, and this one was solidly constructed besides. Back in his younger days, he'd have no trouble dragging the thing high onto the beach. Now, he had to dig his feet deep into the sand and heave with all his strength.

Age was a demon, a haunting that slipped into the bones whispering weakness and frailty. It stole his muscles, his agility, and the quickness of his wit. It seemed a miserable reward for surviving, all things told, which was proof enough that life was a fool's bargain.

Maybe there was a god out there, somewhere, who'd decided that life was a good thing, and so made it real, like blowing on a spark to keep it going until it was nothing but ash, then sitting back and thinking, *Why, that was a worthy thing, wasn't it? Here, let's make lots more!* But a man's spark, or a woman's for that matter, had to be worth more than just a brief flicker of light in the darkness.

Behind him, as he pushed forward step by step, the boat ground its way up from the waves.

The muscles remembered younger, bolder days, and the bones could mutter all they wanted to, and if the haunting aches returned on the morrow, well, he would damn that day when it came.

His back to the sea, working as he was, Whuffine did not see the bloodred sail appear on the southern horizon.

"The challenges of governance," said Bauchelain, studying the wine in the crystal goblet he held up to candelight, "pose unique travails that few common folk have the intelligence to understand. Would you not agree to this, sir?"

"I have said as much many times," Fangatooth replied, glancing over at Coingood. "As you have noted in my Tome of Tyranny, Scribe. Do you see, Bauchelain, how he writes down all that we say? I am assembling a book, you see, a work of many parts, and now, with this night, you yourself enter the narrative of my rise to power."

"How congenial, sir," Bauchelain said, raising the goblet in a toast.

"And if your companion would deign to speak, then he too would be rewarded with immortality, there upon the vellum of my virtues—Coingood, note that one! My vellum of virtues! It's my gift for the turn of phrase, you see, which I am adamant in preserving for posterity. 'Preserving for posterity!' Write that, Scribe!"

"Alas," said Bauchelain, "Korbal Broach's talents lie elsewhere, and as a dinner guest he is often noted for his modesty, and his evident appreciation of fine food. Is that not so, my friend?"

Korbal Broach glanced up from his plate. He licked his greasy lips and said, "Those bodies I left outside should be frozen by now, don't you think, Bauchelain?"

"I imagine so," Bauchelain replied.

Grunting, Korbal returned to his meal.

Fangatooth gestured and a servant refilled his goblet. "It always astonishes me," he said, "that so many common people look with horror and revulsion upon a corpse, when I admit to seeing in its lifeless pose a certain eloquence."

"A singular statement, yes."

"Precisely. Flesh in its most artless expression."

"Which transcends the mundane and becomes art itself, when one considers its ongoing potential."

"Potential, yes." Fangatooth then frowned. "What potential do you mean, Bauchelain?"

"Well, take those bodies you suspend upon hooks on your keep wall. Are they not symbolic? Else, why display them at all? The corpse is the purest symbol of authority there is, I would assert. Proof of the power of life over death, and in the face of that, defiance loses all meaning. Resistance becomes a pointless plunge into the lime pit of lost causes."

Throughout this Fangatooth was making rolling gestures with his hand, almost in the scribe's face, and Coingood scratched away as fast as he could.

"The corpse, my friend," continued Bauchelain, "is the truth of power laid bare. Undisguised, stripped away of all obfuscation. Why, the corpse exists in all forms of governance. May it rest beneath soft velvet, or perch gilded in gold, or holding aloft gem-studded swords, it remains a most poignant, if silent, rebuke to all those absurd notions of equality so common among troublemakers." Bauchelain paused and sipped at his wine. "The corpse can only be the friend of the one in power. Like a bedmate, a cold lover, a bony standard, a throne of clammy flesh." He lifted his goblet. "Shall we toast the corpse, my friends?"

From the far end of the table, Emancipor belched and said, "Aye, Master, that's one to drink to, all right."

Fangatooth paused with his goblet almost touching his lips, and turned to eye Emancipor. "Good Bauchelain, you permit your manservant such crass interruptions?"

"I do indulge him, it is true," Bauchelain replied. "With respect to the subject at hand, however, Mister Reese is something of an expert. Among the sailing community, he is known as Mancy the Luckless, for the misfortune that plagues his maritime ventures. Is that not so, Mister Reese?"

"Aye, Master. Me and the sea, we're uneasy bedmates all right. I'll have some more of that wine there, if you please."

"Yet," Bauchelain resumed, "you do seem out of sorts, Mister Reese. Have you caught a chill, perhaps?"

"Chill? Aye, Master, down to the white roots of my hoary soul, but it ain't nothing a little drink won't fix. Lord Fangatooth, thank you for the escort you provided me up here. I doubt I would have survived otherwise."

"Trouble in the village?" Bauchelain inquired.

"Some, Master, but I got away and that's all that counts."

"Dear Mister Reese," said Fangatooth, "I do apologize if you have been in some manner inconvenienced in Spendrugle."

"Milord, some things no man should ever see, and when he does, why, decades of his life are swept away from his future. This is the shiver that takes the bones, the shadow of Hood himself, and it leaves a man stumbling, for a time. So, for the warm fire and the full belly, and all this wine here, I do thank you."

"Well said," Bauchelain added, nodding.

Seemingly mollified, Fangatooth smiled.

Emancipor leaned back, as the conversation at the other end of the table returned to its discussion of tyranny and whatnot. Against his own will, he thought back, with a shiver, to what he had seen in Feloovil's bedroom. Those mouths had to have come from other people, other women. Cut off and sewn back on . . . but then, he'd seen teeth, and tongues. No, he decided, something wasn't right there.

Pulling out his pipe, he tamped rustleaf into the bowl. Moments later, through clouds of smoke, he studied the scribe, Coingood. Scratching and scribbling, working through one wax tablet after another, the contents of which he'd then, presumably, transfer onto his lord's vellum of virtues. A life trapped in letters seemed a frightful thing, and one at the behest of a madman probably had few high points. No, Emancipor was glad he was not in Coingood's place.

Far better, obviously, this life of his, as manservant to a madman and his equally mad companion. Frowning, Emancipor reached for the nearest decanter of wine. *That's what's wrong with everything. It's the mad who are in charge. Who decided that was a good idea? The gods, I suppose, but they're madder than all the rest. We live under the jumpy heel of insanity, is what we do, and is it any wonder we drink, and worse?*

At the far end of the table, the madmen were smiling, even Korbal Broach.

I think I want to kill someone.

". . . a most fascinating principle," his master was saying. "Are you absolutely consistent, sir, in hanging every stranger who visits your demesne?"

"For the most part," Fangatooth replied. "I do make exceptions, of course. Hence your presence here, as my guests."

"Now, sir," said Bauchelain with a faint tilt of his head, "you are being disingenuous."

"Excuse me?"

Through his smile, Korbal Broach said, "You poisoned our food."

"Yellow paralt," said Bauchelain, nodding. "Fortunately, both Korbal and I are long since inured to that particular poison."

Emancipor choked on his wine. He struggled to his feet, clutching the sides of his head. "I'm poisoned?"

"Relax," said Bauchelain, "I have been lacing your rustleaf with various poisons for some months now, Mister

Reese. You are quite hale, as much as a man who daily imbibes all manner of poisons can be, of course."

Emancipor fell back into his chair. "Oh. Well, that's all right then." He puffed hard on his pipe, glaring at Fangatooth.

The lord was sitting rather still. Then he slowly set his goblet down. "I assure you," he said, "I had no idea. I will have words with my cook."

"As you must," said Bauchelain, rising. "But not before, I hope, I am able to visit this fine kitchen of yours. I still wish to do some baking tonight, and I do promise you, I have no interest in poisoning such efforts, and indeed will prove it to you at first opportunity, by eating any morsel you care to select from my plate of delectable offerings." He rubbed at his hands, smiling broadly. "Why, I feel like a child again!"

"Alas," said Fangatooth, and there was sweat on his high brow, "I regret this breach of trust between us."

"No need, sir. It is forgotten, I assure you. Is that not correct, Korbal?"

"What?"

"The poison."

"What about it? I want to go look at the bodies now." He paused and sniffed, and then said, "A witch used to live here."

Fangatooth blinked. "Indeed, some while back. Witch Hurl was her name. How extraordinary, Korbal, that you can still detect some essence of what must be the faintest of auras."

"What?"

"That you can still smell her, I meant."

"Who? Bauchelain, will there be icing on the cookies?"

"Of course, my friend."

"Good. I like icing."

Moments later, a shaky Lord Fangatooth escorted Bauchelain to the kitchens, while Korbal Broach drew on his heavy cloak and set out for the gates, still smiling.

Emancipor poured some more wine and eyed the scribe. "Coingood, is it?"

The poor man was rubbing his writing hand. The glance he shot at Emancipor was guarded. "Your masters—who in Hood's name are they?"

"Adventurers, I suppose you could call them. There's others names for them, of course, but that's of no matter to me. I get paid, I stay alive, and life could be worse."

Abruptly the scribe thumped the table. "My thoughts exactly! We got to do what we got to do, right?"

"Aye. It ain't pretty, but then, we'd never say it was, would we?"

"Precisely, friend, precisely!"

"Join me, will you? Here, some more wine, assuming it's not poisoned, too."

"Of course not! That would be a terrible waste. Why, I will join you, friend. Why not? Let them bake, or whatever."

"Aye, bake. My master does indeed love to bake."

Shuffling over, Coingood shook his head. "Seems an odd thing to me, I admit."

Oh friend, that makes two of us, believe me. "He is full of surprises, is Bauchelain."

"Fangatooth will draw and quarter the cook, you know."

"For poisoning us, or failing at it?"

Coingood grinned, but said nothing.

Emancipor found a spare goblet and poured the man a glass. Then he lifted his own. "Here's to minions."

"Good! Yes! To minions!"

"The hapless and the helpless."

They drank.

Vague motion through the iced-over window caught Spilgit's eye and he leaned closer.

"More guests?" Ackle the Risen asked, leaning from one foot to the other. The front of his body was warm to the touch, but the back of his body, so close to the mis-aligned door, was frigid. When Spilgit made no reply, Ackle continued, "We're in the same boat, my friend. Simply, we need to get out of Spendrugle. Now, winter's a hard season in these here parts, I'll grant you. But one of the Carter's better wagons, a solid ox or two, and plenty of food, rum and furs, and we could make it to a city on the coast inside a week, or we head north, though the roads will be bad, and the winds—"

"For a supposed dead man, Ackle, you talk way too much."

"What so fascinates you out there, then?"

"Three strangers."

"They're back? From the keep? Why—"

"Not them, you fool. Three other strangers. One of them's all bandaged about the head, and limping. An-other one's a woman, half naked and that's the half I can't take my eyes off."

Ackle swung round and tugged open the door. He peered out. "A gull got one of her tits," he said.

"That's a birthmark, idiot."

"Too white for that."

"Ain't no gulls, Ackle. Too cold for gulls. No, it's a lack of pigment. Seen the like before, only not there, on the tit, I mean."

The three strangers continued on to stop in front of the

King's Heel. They argued there for a moment, in some foreign language, and then went inside.

"Wonder if Hordilo's going to arrest them?"

Spilgit sat back in his chair and sighed, rubbing at his eyes. "Might need a golem to do that. They were all armed."

Ackle pushed the door shut as much as it was possible to do so, and then faced the tax collector again. "We could buy us a wagon and an ox, and stores and all, even for three of us, Spilgit, if you want to take Felittle. We could leave in the morning."

"Oh, and how will we pay for all that? Carter's no fool and won't give credit."

Ackle smiled. "Let's find us a pair of shovels, shall we?"

"Oh, not this buried treasure rubbish again!"

"I wasn't about to leave on my own, not with the cold and all. But now, well, here you are, Spilgit, with Feloo-vil planning to kill you a hundred ways. It's only indecision that's stayed her hand so far. As for Felittle, well, you should've heard her have a go at her ma. Things were said. Things there's no going back on. If you want her, now's the time, friend."

"Friend? You're not my friend."

"Then partner."

"I don't partner with men who think they're dead."

"Why not? I imagine there's some tax break involved."

Spilgit studied Ackle for a long moment, and then shook his head. "Shovels. Fine, we'll get some shovels. We'll dig up your treasure and then snatch Felittle away and make Carter rich and then make our getaway. What a plan. Pure genius."

"Genius isn't required," Ackle replied, "when it's all straightforward, like I've been saying."

Spilgit rose and collected up his threadbare cloak. "You never had the look of a wealthy man, Ackle."

"Never got the chance, Spilgit. Now, where will we get some shovels?"

"Gravedigger's place," Spilgit replied. "We'll offer to dig him a few holes, what with all the strangers about, and we'll offer it cheap."

Ackle hesitated. "I don't like that man."

"You should. You should bless the drunk every damned dawn and every damned sunset."

"We're not on speaking terms, is what I mean."

Spilgit stared. "I'll get the shovels, then."

"I appreciate it, Spilgit. I really do. I'll wait here."

"If you're wasting my time, Ackle . . ."

"I'm not. You'll see."

When Spilgit had left, Ackle moved round the small desk and sat in the chair. He spent a moment imagining himself as a tax collector, stuffy with official whatever, feared by all and charmed on every turn by those same horrible people. He let the scenes linger in his head, and then sighed. "No, I'd rather be dead."

Hordilo was sick of escorting fools up to the keep. He was sick, in fact, of the whole thing. His responsibilities, the blood on his hands, the pointless repetition of it all, and the way every day ahead of him, down to the last day of his life, was probably going to be no different from all the days already behind him.

Most men dreamed the same things: a warm body to lie against, echoing their animal grunts; company at mealtimes; decent conversation and the floor free of scraps. But few men imagined a woman might want the same things, and then find them in a dog.

Wives were a curse, no doubt about it. So Hordilo had learned to trim down his dreams, as befitted a man made wise by years of grief and blissful ignorance horribly shattered on a fateful day when the world turned on its head and blew him a mocking kiss. It all came down to avoiding the pitfalls awaiting a decent man wanting a decent life, but that was never as easy as it should be.

He sat glowering at the table, ignoring the moans and complaints from all the scratched-up fools who'd been too slow or too drunk to escape the claws of Red the lizard cat, and studied the three newcomers lined up at the bar.

Now, a woman like that one would do me fine. She don't mind her mostly nakedness, I see, and showing me that backside ain't no accident, since I'm the only good-looking man in here and she eyed me coming in. Too knowing to be cold. Why, she could thaw a snared rabbit under hip-deep snow. And make it jump, at least once.

But no, he'd have to arrest her. Along with her two companions, and then see them all hanged until dead. What lord made a law that said being a stranger was against the law? The death sentence for having an unfamiliar face seemed a little harsh, as far as punishments went.

The three were speaking with Feloovil, but she was only half-listening, dabbing a damp cloth against the rake of claw-marks running down her right cheek. Finally, with an irritated gesture she indicated Hordilo and the three strangers swung round.

The bandaged one limped over. "You! You thook them up there? The keep? And they wath made guethth?"

Hordilo glared at the other two. "You elected this one your spokesman?"

The woman scowled. "Bauchelain and Korbal Broach, and Mancy the Luckless. They're all up at the keep, are they?"

"They are, and you're welcome to join them."

"Thath awfully nithe of you," the bandaged man said, nodding and smiling.

"Just take the track up to the gate and knock," said Hordilo, waving one hand. Then he pointed at the woman. "But not you."

"Why not me?"

"Got to question you."

"About what?"

"I'm the one asking the questions, not you. Now, get over here and sit. You two, go on, up to the keep. There'll be a fine meal awaiting you, I'm sure."

"And her?" the third man asked, nodding at the woman.

"I'll send her up anon."

"Go on," said the woman to her companions. "He's the law around here."

"I uphold the law," Hordilo corrected her. "It's Lord Fangatooth's law."

"Lord what?"

"Fangatooth. You all think that's funny? Go and tell him so, then."

When the two men had finished their drinks and left,

the woman carried her tankard over and sat down opposite Hordilo. She studied him with level eyes and that was a look Hordilo knew all too well.

"Is that what you think?" he asked in a growl.

"Why shouldn't I?' she retorted, slouching and setting her tankard down on the thigh of the lone leg she stretched out—the one bare and pale and with a delicious curved line where the meat of it slung down from the chair's edge, and the sight of that made Hordilo want to fall to his hands and knees and crawl up under that thigh, if only to feel its weight on the back of his neck. He shifted about, felt sweat everywhere under his clothing.

"I don't like it when women think that," he said.

One brow arched. "If you weren't that way then no woman would think it, would she?"

"I wasn't until some woman did me in, not that I was ever married, of course, but if I had been, why, she would've done me in, all because she was thinking what she was thinking."

"You're blaming the water for the hole it fills."

"I've just seen that too many times," Hordilo said, feeling surly. "Women thinking."

"If that's what you think, why talk to me? You could've questioned Gust Hubb, or Heck, even. But you didn't.

You picked me, on account of me being a woman. So let's face it, you keep making the same mistakes in your life and I ain't to blame for that, am I?"

"If we're talking blame here," Hordilo retorted, "then it was you that sat down thinking what you were thinking. I ain't blind and I ain't dumb and I don't take kindly to being thought of that way, when we only just met."

"What's your name?"

"Hordilo. Captain Hordilo."

"All right, Captain Hordilo, since you know what I'm thinking, what are we doing here?"

"Women always think I'm that easy, don't they."

"Is that what I was thinking?"

"I know what you were thinking, so don't try and slip around it with all this talk of us taking a room upstairs to continue this conversation. I got laws to uphold. Responsibilities. You're a stranger, after all."

"You only think I'm a stranger," she replied, "because you ain't got to know me yet."

"Of course you're a stranger. I never seen you before. Nobody has, nobody around here, I mean. I don't even know your name."

"Birds Mottle."

"That hardly matters," he replied.

"Yes it does. Strangers don't have names, not names you'd know, I mean. But I do, and you know it."

"What were you thinking, showing me that leg of yours?"

She glanced down and frowned. "I wasn't showing it to you. I was just letting it lie there, resting. It does that when I sit."

"I ain't fooled by anything so obvious," Hordilo replied. He reached down and held his hand under her thigh. He hefted it once, then twice. "That's a decent feel, I think."

"You think?"

"I know. Decent weight. Solid, but soft, too." He moved it up and down a few more times.

"Looks like something you'd be happy doing all day," Birds Mottle noted.

Sighing, Hordilo sat back. "And you said you didn't think I knew what you were thinking."

"Got me."

He rose. "All right, then."

"Upstairs?"

"I get this all the time," he said, "for being so handsome."

Her eyes widened. But he'd seen that look, too, plenty of times, and whatever she was thinking, why, she could keep it to herself.

. . .

Feloovil Generous watched the two head up to Hordilo's room. She shook her head. There was no telling the tastes of women, and of all the idiotic conversations she'd heard from Hordilo over the years, that one was close to tops. *Can't figure how he does it. How it works every damned time.*

We'll still see her hang, of course. So, I guess, everyone wins.

She patted the stinging slashes on her cheek, looked round to see if Felittle had cracked open the cellar door and slipped out, but even as her head turned she saw the door snap shut again, the latch thrown with a muted *thunk.* Good, that embarrassment from her own womb could rot down there, for all Feloovil cared.

In the rooms above—all the rooms barring the one now occupied by Hordilo and that slutty woman—all of her girls were weeping and trying to put together what was left of them. Someone would have to sweep up the clumps of hair and bits of skin, but that could wait on her lovelies repairing themselves with makeup and wigs and whatnot.

She'd warned her daughter about taking in that lizard cat. It might have shown up looking half-dead and with a witless look in its wandering eyes, but a wild creature was just that. It belonged out among the rocks, sliming across the cliff-faces above the waves eating birds and eggs and stuff, instead of killing and eating the village cats and some of the dogs, too.

A spasm of grief clutched her at the thought of the two dogs Red had torn open. Scurry and Tremble had been decent hounds, a little fat and slow, true—fatally so, it turned out—and now Wriggle was all alone and pining under Ackle's table . . . and where had that stinking man gone to? He should have been back by now, with Spilgit in tow, which would have given her the opportunity to turn this miserable day right around.

Throat-cut tax collectors stung no tears in any village. Questions of vengeance didn't need utterance, in fact, as it was more or less a given. She could picture a score of indifferent shrugs, and maybe a low quip about how Hood, Lord of Death, was the biggest tax collector of them all, or some such thing. A justifiable murder, then.

She should never have trusted Ackle with the task.

The door opened again and in strode three more strangers.

The man in the lead, carrying in both hands a huge sword, fixed Feloovil with a glare and in a ferocious accent said, "Where are they, then?"

"Up at the keep," she replied. "Everyone's up at the

keep, and there they'll stay, for as long as the Lord wants to entertain 'em. Now you three, you look worn out and all. So put those weapons away and sit down and I'll check the cookpot."

They stared at her for a moment, and then the man with the sword sheathed it and turned to his companions. "Like Wormlick said, we're almost there. Time for a celebratory drink."

The other man—the third one was a woman, slinky and evil-looking—edged up to Feloovil where she stood behind the bar. His beard could not hide the mottled rings on his face, and he was eyeing the stairs and licking his lips.

The first man asked, "You got girls for hire, then?"

"For you, aye," she replied. "But not the one with ringworm. Got to take care of my girls, right?"

The man glanced over at his companion and shrugged.

"Always the way," the ringwormed man said in a grumble. "Never mind. You go on, Bisk. Take two and think of me."

The man named Bisk made a face. "Thinking of you won't do me any good, Wormlick, if you know what I mean." He then strode to the stairs and clambered up them as if he was one short cousin away from an ape.

The woman sidled up beside Wormlick. "Don't get

down on yourself," she said to him. "Things could always be worse."

"So you keep saying," Wormlick replied, and then caught Feloovil's eye. "You, ale and food, like you promised!"

"And here I was starting to feel sorry for you," Feloovil said, heading off to check the new pot of stew on its hook above the hearth.

"Yeah?" Wormlick called out behind her. "Maybe I'll just take what I want and damn to you, then! What do you think of that?"

"Go ahead and try," she replied, "and you'll never leave the Heel alive."

"Who'd stop me?"

She faced him. "I would, you rude pocked oaf. Don't test me 'cause I ain't in the mood. Now, d'you want to eat and drink in here? Fine, only pay up first, on account of you not being local and all." She collected up a couple of bowls, filled them both with broth and then spat in one before turning to walk back to the strangers.

But the woman was standing right in front of her. She took up the bowl not spat in and said, "This one will do me fine, love, and wine if you have it."

Feloovil watched the woman sway her way back to the

bar. *Now that's what a good daughter should be like. Except for the evil eyes, of course. But then, at least evil implies some kind of intelligence. Ah, Felittle, it's all your father's fault, may his bones rot.*

Smiling, she carried the other bowl to Wormlick.

Whuffine sat back down in his chair, listening to the wind start its moan outside. Beneath lowered lids he studied the hunched lizard cat in the cage. "So you ran to the old cave, did you? Made a mess of your cozy life in the tavern and had to get out quick." He shook his head. "But that cave ain't yours no more," he told the creature. "It's mine, for my stores. Not even consecrated any more, since I made a point of breaking the idols and scattering the offerings into the sea. It's . . . what's the word? Desecrated."

The cat glared at him in the manner of all cats, its scaly tail twitching like a tentacle.

"So I set the trap," he continued, "knowing you'd be back sooner or later. Now here you are," he finished with a sigh, "the ninth. The last of you."

Red hissed at him.

"Enough of that, Hurl. Your witching nights are done

with, now. For good. You was killing too many locals, not to mention their livestock. It couldn't go on. I'm a patient man, a tolerant man, even, and minding my own business *is* my business. But you went and got greedy." He shook his head. "Now it's the cliff for you, Witch."

He rose, pulling on his fox-fur hat and collecting up his walking stick and then, in one hand, the chains looped through the bars of the cage. Kicking open the door, he dragged the cage outside, and onto the cliff trail that climbed to the lesser of the two promontories. The light was fading but the air had grown wild and he could hear the frenzy of the waves as they pounded the rocks down and to his right.

As the cage scraped and growled its way up the trail in Whuffine's wake, Hurl lunged against the sides, spat and bounced and cracked its head; its limbs shot out between the iron bars and slashed at Whuffine, but the chains were long and he remained beyond the lizard cat's reach.

He was breathing hard by the time he reached the half-floor of tiles that marked the summit of the promontory— the other half had tumbled down to the broken shore below a century back, maybe more, and nothing else remained of the temple that had once commanded this grisly view. But he remembered that ghastly edifice, and the way it crouched like an ape, its gnarled face peering across the bay's surly waters to Wurms Keep. He doubted even Hood knew the name of the temple's long forgotten god or goddess.

The windswept floor of worn tiles bore the faded, tessellated image of something demonic, its horror peculiarly blunted by the seemingly laughing cherubs half-hanging out of its fanged mouth. Miserable faith for a miserable place: it was hardly surprising how those two meshed with such perfection, and could make nightmares out of what could have been simple lives. He suspected that bad weather was the cause of most evil in the world. Gods just showed up to give a face to the foul madness. People had the need for such things, he knew, the poor fools.

He dragged the cage round until it balanced precariously on the cliff's edge. Dropping the chains and keeping his distance, Whuffine walked out to look down at the thrashing chaos of the rocks and spume below. "Your sisters and brothers are waiting down there," he said to the cat. "Or at least their bones are. I never liked shapeshifters, you know, and D'ivers are the worst of them all. But I would've tolerated you, darling. I would have. So it's just too bad you got to end like this."

The lizard cat wailed.

"I know," he said, nodding, "you've barely the wits left

to even know who you was. Not my problem, of course, but I think it makes this something of a mercy, at least for the witch, if not for the brainless cat." He looked down at the caged creature. "So long, Hurl."

He went round until the cage was between him and the cliff edge, and then jumped forward and gave it a hard kick.

The cat howled.

Chains whipping across the tiles, the cage slipped from sight and plunged to the rocks far below.

Whuffine stepped closer to the edge and peered down in time to see it strike. In the instant before the mangled cage slid down beneath the waves, he saw that its door was swinging wildly. There was a flash of motion, weasel-like, and then nothing. "Ah," murmured Whuffine. "Shit."

Glancing up, he saw a huge, battered ship lunging into the bay, appearing so suddenly he would have sworn it had been conjured by the storm itself. Racing past the cut, it churned through the swells and, with a terrible sound that reached Whuffine atop the cliff, the hull drove into the sand. Waves exploded over its stern. The masts snapped and on their red billowing sails lifted into the air as the gale sought to carry everything into the sky. A moment later, amidst whipping lines, the rigging fell like a crimson shroud into the foaming seas.

Upon the canted deck, figures were swarming.

Whuffine sighed. "What a busy day." Picking up his walking stick, he set out on the trail, down to meet these newcomers.

Gust Hubb sat on a rock, hands over his bandaged ears as he rocked back and forth. He made low moaning sounds that the wind answered with glee.

Heck scowled at the man for a moment longer and then turned to look up at the keep. "I don't like the looks of that place," he said. "And somehow, Gust, now it's just you and me, I'm thinking the farther away we are from those necromancers—and Mancy the Luckless—the safer we'll be."

"They owe uth!" Gust said, looking up, his working eye wild with the whites showing all around. "They owe me a healing! Ath leatht that! Look at me, Heck! Lithen to me! I want my tongue whole athain! It wath all their faulth!"

The wind was fierce and bitterly cold. Rain filled with sea spray was spitting into their faces: proof to Heck's mind that the world didn't think too much of them, and didn't give a Hood's heel about justice and making things right. It was all one long slog up some damned storm-whipped trail to some damned tower with some damned light shining and offering the false promise of warm salvation. That was life, wasn't it? As pointless as praying. As meaningless as dying when dying was all there was, somewhere up ahead, maybe closer than anyone'd like, but then, wasn't it always closer than anyone'd like, no matter when that was? Well, it felt close enough right now, and if Gust was aching and moaning and too gimpy to finish this cursed climb, why, Heck wouldn't complain too much, and might even secretly confess—to someone, but no one nearby—that it was a whisker's trim from death where they were right now, and one step up the wrong way would see their bodies cold and lifeless before the dawn.

No, he wasn't sorry Gust was all done in, the poor man. Taking those necromancers aboard in Lamentable Moll had been the worst decision in Sater's life, and the captain had paid for it with that life, and now the *Suncurl* was a gnawed, burnt and chewed-up wreck, a sad end for the only ship to ever mate with a dhenrabi. *Some things, it has to be said, just aren't worth seeing close up, and that's all I'll say on the matter.*

"Whereth Birdth?" Gust asked.

"Probably rolling in the furs with that sheriff," Heck said, and just saying those words out loud made him feel suicidal. "She's a love no man can hold on to," he said morosely. "It's my curse—maybe yours, too, Gust, the way she was eyeing that split tongue of yours—to love the wrong woman."

"Oh, thut up, Heck."

"No, really. I wish I was the kind of man who could look at a woman's naked body and say, 'nice, but it ain't enough, 'cause you ain't got the rest, so whatever it is you want from me, why, you ain't gonna get it.' If I was a man like that, appreciative and all, but with, well, with *standards*, I bet I'd be a happier man."

Gust had dropped his hands and was staring up at Heck with his one good eye. "We need to thave her."

"From what? She's exactly where she wants to be!"

"But thath theriff wuth ugly!"

"Aye, ugly in that gods-awful lucky way some ugly men have, when it comes to women. Now, good-looking men, with those winning smiles and good skin and whatnot, well, I wish 'em all the evil luck the world can bring, but luckily, we're not talking about them." He shook his head. "It don't matter anyway, Gust. She's happy and it's a happy without you or me and that's what stings."

Hearing boots crunching on the trail below both turned, momentarily hopeful, until it was clear that there was more than one person coming up on them, and as the newcomers came round a twist in the trail, stepping out from behind an outcrop, Gust rose to stand beside Heck, and both men stared in disbelief.

"You're alive!" Heck shouted.

Bisk Fatter drew out his sword. "Aye, and we got a thing about being betrayed, Heck Urse."

"Not uth!" Gust cried.

Wormlick asked, "That you, Gust Hubb? Gods below, what happened to you?"

"Forget it," snapped Bisk, hefting the sword. "We ain't no Mowbri's Choir here, Wormlick, so save the songs of sympathy."

"I'll say," said Sordid, revealing a thin-bladed dagger in one hand and setting its point to the nails of the other in quick succession. "You never could sing, anyway."

Wormlick glared at her. "What would you know about it? I wouldn't sing for you if you held my cock in one hand and that knife in the other!"

She laughed. "Oh yes you would, if I asked sweetly."

"How did you survive?" Heck asked them.

"We shucked off our armour and swam to the damned surface, you fool! But you were already under way, vanishing in the night!"

"Not that," Heck said. "I meant, how did you survive

in each other's company since then? You all hate each other!"

"Treachery carves a deeper hate than the hate you're talking about, Heck. Now, we're here for our cut and then we're cutting you."

"Ththill the idiot, eh, Bithk? Why would we cut you in on anything if you're then going to kill uth?"

"That's just talk," said Sordid. "He wasn't supposed to tell you we're going to kill you until *after* you gave us our cut. That's what you get from a fifty-six-year-old corporal."

"And you take my orders!" Bisk retorted. "Making you even dumber!"

"I'll accept that for the truth you just admitted to, sir."

As Bisk Fatter frowned and tried to work out what she'd just said, Heck Urse cleared his throat and said, "Listen, there wasn't no cut. We lost it all."

"We never had ith in the firthth plathe," Gust added, sitting back down and clutching the side of his head again.

"Sater's dead," Heck continued.

"Birds?" Sordid asked.

Heck's shoulders slumped. "Not you, too?" He sighed. "She's alive, down in that inn down there." He gestured at the keep. "We picked up a cargo of trouble in Lamentable

Moll, and we were just on our way to demand, er, compensation. Look at Gust. That's what those bastards did to us."

"What bastards?" Sordid asked, her sleepy eyes suddenly sharp.

"Necromanthers," said Gust. "And if thath wuthn't enouthff, they got Manthy the Thluckthleth with 'em!"

"And you want compensation?" Sordid laughed, sheathing her knife. "Corporal, we chased these idiots across the damned ocean. It really is a contest in stupidity here, and this squad you're now commanding could crush an army of optimists with nary a blink." Turning, she stared out to sea, started and then said, "Oh, look, here come the Chanters."

Her next laugh shriveled Heck's sack down to the size of a cocoon.

With two ashen-faced servants dragging the dead cook away by the feet, Lord Fangatooth grasped hold of Coingood's arm and pulled him out through the doorway, leaving Bauchelain and his manservant in the steamy kitchen.

"Did you write it all down?"

"Of course, milord—"

"Every word? And who said what?"

Coingood nodded, trying to keep from trembling while still in the clutches of his lord, and the hand encircling his upper arm was spotted with blood, since it was the hand that had driven a knife through the cook's left eye.

"Find the clever things he said, Scribe, and change them around."

"Milord?"

"I'm the only one who says clever things, you fool! Make it so I said them—is that too complicated an order for you to comprehend?"

"No, milord. Consider it done!"

"Excellent!" Fangatooth hissed. "Now, walk with me. Leave them to their baking—"

"He'll poison it, milord—"

"No he won't. He's too subtle, and that's what all this was about—making me look clumsy and oafish. That damned cook! Well, he won't be messing things up anymore, will he?"

"No, milord. But . . . who will make the meals?"

"Find someone else. None of that matters now. We need to devise a way of killing them. But cleverly, just to show them. We need genius here, Scribe!"

"But milord, it's—well, it's not in my nature to think diabolically."

Fangatooth shook him. "You think the way I tell you to think!"

"Yes, milord!"

Lord Fangatooth held up his fist and said, "This is a game of murder, my friend, and I mean to win it or die trying!"

Emancipor found a jug the contents of which smelled vaguely alcoholic. He downed a mouthful, and then another. The taste was sweet, cloying, and it burned his throat and made his sinuses drain down the back of his mouth, and then his eyes started watering fiercely. Grunting, he drank some more.

"Power that lacks subtlety," said Bauchelain as he gathered and began lining up a half-dozen wooden bowls of varying sizes, "betrays a failure of the intellect. Do you think, Mister Reese, it is safe to say that our host lacks certain nuances, degrading the very notion of tyranny? The veil is absent. Sleight of hand unimagined. The obfuscation of language and the unspoken threat are revealed as, well, let's be honest, as unexplored realms in this lord's mind. All of this, I must admit, is disappointing."

"Well, master, this is a backwater holding, after all."

"There is grit in this flour," Bauchelain said. "A millstone needs replacing. I am afraid I made no note of the dentition of our host or his servants, but I imagine we would see teeth worn down, chipped and gouged. Backwater indeed, Mister Reese, as you say." Dusting his hands, he stepped over to Emancipor and gently pried the jug from Reese's hand. "Extract of the vanilla bean, Mister Reese, is rather expensive. I believe you have already drunk down a month's wages, so it is well that the cook is no longer alive to witness such sacrilege."

"Master, my stomach is on fire."

"I imagine it would be. Will you survive?'

"No."

"Your pessimism has lost whatever charm it once possessed, Mister Reese."

"Must be all the poisons, Master, squirreling my brain. Thing is, everywhere I look, or even think of looking, I see doom and disaster, hoary and leering. Shades in every corner and heavy clouds overhead. I ain't known good luck in so long I'd not know the lad's face if it up and kissed me." He set about finding another jug. He needed something to quell the fires in his gut.

"Do you like cookies, Mister Reese?"

"Depends, Master."

"Upon what?"

"What I been smoking, of course."

"I suggest that you constrain your blends, Mister Reese, to simple rustleaf."

"You don't want me to eat your cookies, Master? I thought you said you weren't going to poison them."

Bauchelain sighed. "Ah, Mister Reese, perhaps I only wish to see them shared out fairly among our hosts. It is, after all, the least we can do for their hospitality."

"Master, they tried to kill us."

Bauchelain snorted. "It is a kindness calling such crude efforts an attempt to kill us. Tell me, do you know how to make icing?"

Emancipor scratched at his whiskers, and then shrugged. "Seen the wife do it enough times, so, aye, I suppose."

"Ah, your wife baked?"

"No, she just made icing. In a big bowl, and then ate it all herself, usually in one night. Once a month, every month. Who can fathom the mind of a woman, eh, Master? Or even a wife."

"Not any man, surely. Or husband."

Emancipor nodded. "That's a fact, Master. Mind you, I doubt most women can fathom each other, either. They're like cats that way. Or sharks. Or those river fish with all the sharp teeth. Or crocodiles, or snakes in a pit. Or wasps—"

"Mister Reese, do get on with that icing, will you? Korbal Broach so loves icing."

"Sweet tooth, then."

"I suppose it shows," Bauchelain said in a tolerant murmur. "So like a child, is my companion."

Emancipor thought about that, conjuring in his mind Korbal's broad, round face, the flabby lips, the pallor and the small, shallow eyes. He then thought about children, envisaging a toddling Korbal Broach running in a pack of runts, big-toothed smile and a snippet of hair on that now bald head. He shuddered. *The fools. They should've known. One look, and they should've known. Those kind you do away with, head in a bucket, left out in the snows overnight, accidentally mixed up with the dog food, don't matter how, you just do away with them, and if the world trembles to your crime, relax, that was the rattle of relief.* Aye, that boy running with his gang, a gang that kept getting smaller, with all those pale parents wondering where their children vanished to, and there stood young Korbal Broach, face empty and eyes emptier. *They should've known. Priests can't cure them, sages can't unlearn them, jailers don't want them.*

Bundle him in a sack of lard and raw meat and dump

the whole mess into a pit of starving dogs, aye. But who am I fooling? Children like Korbal never die. Only the nice ones die, and for that alone the world deserves every damned curse a decent soul could utter. "Master?"

"Mister Reese?"

"You done with that vanilla?"

"That's right," said Spilgit, "two shovels."

Gravedigger looked up blearily from the heap of dead people's clothes that he'd sewn together to make a mattress and pillow. "That's *my* job," he said, reaching for the clay jug, his arm snaking out like a withered root to tangle hairy fingers in the jug's ear, then drag it across the floor back to his bed.

"You look settled in, friend," said Spilgit. "I've been temporarily barred from the Heel, you see, and well, a man needing to stay warm has to work. Physical work, I mean."

"You gonna use a shovel in each hand, then?"

"That's a silly idea, isn't it?"

"Right. So the other shovel, what's that for? Taxes? You taxing my one shovel and claiming the other as payment?"

"I think you've had a bit too much to drink."

"Too much and what you're saying might make sense. Too bad for you, then, isn't it?"

"Taxation doesn't work that way."

"Yes it does." Gravedigger drank.

"All right, it does work that way. You keep one shovel and the tax collector takes the other one, and uses it to build you a nice level road."

"Oh yeah? So how come it's me building that road, breaking my back and using my own shovel to do it with? While you sit there doing nothing, but you got a key in your pocket, and that's the key to a giant vault full of shovels. So tell me again, what good are you to anyone?"

"This is ridiculous," Spilgit said. "People have different talents. You build roads, or in this case, dig graves, and I do the collecting, or in this case, er, dig the graves."

"Exactly, so take one shovel and go to it."

"But I'd like both shovels."

"Once a tax collector, always a tax collector."

"Listen, you drunk fool! Give me the shovels!"

"I ain't got two shovels. I only got the one."

Spilgit clutched his head. "Why didn't you say so?"

The man tipped the jug again, swallowed, and wiped his mouth. "I just did."

"Where is it?"

"Where's what?"

"Your shovel."

"You tax that shovel away from me and I ain't got no more work, meaning I don't earn nothing, meaning you can't tax a man who don't earn nothing, meaning you're useless. But you know you're useless, don't you, and that's why you want to take up grave digging, so you got yourself a real job, but what about me?"

"Are you going to loan me your shovel or not?"

"Loan now, is it? You gotta pay for that, mister."

"Fine," Spilgit sighed. "How much?"

"Well, seeing as I'm renting the shovel from Hallig the pig trencher, and he's charging me a sliver a dig, for you it'll have to be two slivers, or I don't see any profit for my kindness."

"Kindness means you don't charge anything!"

"I'm a businessman here, Tax Collector."

"If you rent me that shovel, I'll have to tax your earnings."

"How much?"

"A sliver."

"Then I make nothing."

Spilgit shrugged. "I doubt anyone'd ever claim renting shovels was a profit-making enterprise."

"Hallig does."

"Listen, that damned shovel is leaning outside your

front door. I could have come up here and just taken it and you'd never have known the difference."

Gravedigger nodded. "That's a fact."

"But I thought to do this legitimately, as one neighbour to another."

"More fool you."

"I see that," Spilgit snapped.

"Now what, then, Mister Tax Collector?"

"I'm taxing you that shovel."

Gravedigger shrugged. "Go ahead, now it's Hallig's problem. Only the next time you need to bury somebody, don't bother coming to me. I'm now unemployed."

"I'll loan you a shovel from the vault."

"Right, and I suppose you want me to be grateful or something. Is it any wonder tax collectors are despised?"

Spilgit watched the man take another drink, and then he left the shack, collected up the shovel, and then, noticing another shovel beside it, he collected that one too, and headed off.

Red huddled in the wet cave with nothing but bones for company. Just below, down a slant of bedrock, the seas surged with foam and uprooted trees from some tumbled cliff side; and with each thunderous wave Red's refuge grew more precarious as water rolled up and over the rock.

Amidst the racket, the bones jumbled around the cat seemed to whisper, in flinty voices, and he could almost make out the words as he crouched, trembling with fury. The low susurrations filled his skull. He glared at the bones, and saw in the gloom skulls among them. The skulls of lizard cats. They rustled and shifted before his eyes, and the whispering grew more urgent.

Red could smell a whiff of power, old power, and a need gripped his soul like a clawed hand about a throat.

Ssss . . . sssembling!

Semble! Semble you fool!

Yowling, the cat shook with tremors, and the bones crowded close, and things suddenly blurred.

The sorcery made the sweat on the cave walls steam and spit. Stone fissured and fell, shattering. In the miasma surrounding Red, old bones pushed into the cat's body. There was terrible pain, and then triumph.

"I am Hurl! Witch Hurl!"

She tottered to her feet, impossibly weak, and looked down at her naked form. Leathery skin stretched over bones, tendons like twine. Not enough flesh, not enough living tissue to make her whole, to make her as she once was. But, it was *enough*.

Hurl cackled. "I have my mind back! My beautiful, perfect mind! And . . . and . . . I remember everything!" A moment later she slumped. "I remember everything."

She needed food. Fresh meat, hot, bloody meat. She needed to feed, and she needed it *now*.

Feeling frail, she ventured out from the cave, skirting the foaming tumult. It was almost dark, the storm coming in like a bruise on a god's forehead. There were corpses wedged among the rocks. Then she saw one lift an arm. Cackling, Hurl scrambled towards the hapless figure.

But when she crouched over him, she found herself looking down upon a dead man. Who then smiled. "I was never much of a sailor," he said. "Tiny said: take the tiller. I tried to warn him, but the Chanters listen to nobody. I'm stuck. Will you help me?"

"You're dead!" she spat.

"I know, and that's the thing, isn't it? We're all cursed with our lot. I was probably alive once, but it's not like I can go back. No one can. Still, if you help me get out of this crevasse, then I could walk home. It's somewhere across the ocean, but I'll find it, I'm sure. Eventually."

"But I need warm flesh! Hot blood!"

"Don't we all, darling?"

She shook her head. "You'll have to do, for now. It isn't much, but it's something."

"A philosophy we share, my sweet. Now, about this

help—oh, what are you doing? You're eating my thigh. That's not very nice, and you an old woman at that. Well, I suppose if you eat enough of me, I'll be able to squeeze free. So that's something. When you're dead, it pays to remain optimistic, or so I have found. Not too much on that one now, all right? Here, see, you can reach the other one, too. It's much fresher, I'm sure. Horrible weather we're having, isn't it?"

Tiny Chanter turned to survey his surviving siblings as they gathered on the beach, the icy water thrashing up round their ankles as the storm worsened. "It's simple now," he said. "We kill everybody."

The one sister among them, Relish, snorted. "That's your plan, Tiny?"

"That's always my plan."

"Exactly, and see where it's gotten us."

Frowning, Midge said, "It's got us on shore, Relish."

"Like Midge says," growled Tiny, "it's got us here, and that makes it a good plan, just like it's always been a good plan, since it got us wherever we ended up, and we ain't ended up anywhere but where the plan meant us to end up, and if you think I'm going to keep on tolerating your bad moods and foul mouth, Relish, well, that ain't in the plan." He turned to the others. "Draw your weapons, brothers. There's killing to do, and that killing ends with those two sorcerers who stole our treasury."

"They didn't steal our treasury," said Scant. "It was a squad of city guards and that treacherous captain, Sater."

Tiny scowled. "But she's dead, and we had nothing to do with that, meaning we're still hunting for justice, and punishment, and those sorcerers objected to us killing them and that's not allowed. We got to answer for things like that."

Puny Chanter laughed. "Sater got between a dhenrabi and his mate! That was funny!"

Sneering, Relish said, "It's only funny to you, Puny, because you're sick in the head."

"That's funny, too! Hah hah!"

"Be quiet all of you," commanded Tiny. "Draw your damned weapons and let's get on with it. Stint, Fren, Gil, you kill that man up at the shack. But don't mess up that fur cap of his. I want it. The rest of us, we go to the village. We get us a warm meal if we can find it, and maybe a few tankards, and then we kill everyone. Then we go up to that keep and kill everything there, too."

"It's your genius what leaves me speechless," said Relish.

"I wish," Tiny replied. Then he pointed at two of his

brothers who were both gripping the same huge sword. "Flea, Lesser, what in Hood's name are you doing?"

"It's our three-handed sword, Tiny," said Flea.

Tiny walked up to Flea and whacked him on the side of the head. "Let go of that! There, take that axe, the five-bladed one. Let's go everyone, we're in for a bloody night."

They set off up the beach, falling into single file on the trail, with Stint, Fren and Gil taking up the rear.

Leaning on his walking stick, Whuffine Gaggs stood beside his shack and watched the ten strangers approach. They were a big lot, he saw, each one with weapons bared and marching in a way that seemed ominous. Probably Tarthenal blood in the line, somewhere a few generations back. The sight of them made him feel nostalgic. The one woman among them was more reasonably proportioned. In fact, he saw as they drew closer, she had more curves than a clay ball, and knew how to use them as she bounced and rolled her way up the trail.

The one in the lead offered up a bright smile that didn't reach his eyes, and simply trudged past Whuffine, as did all the others barring the last three. They halted and readied their weapons.

Whuffine sighed. "It's like that, is it?"

The one in the centre of the line shrugged. "Tiny says we kill everybody."

"You got me all over nostalgic here," Whuffine said.

The man grinned and turned to the man on his right. "Hear that, Stint? The old comber remembers better days."

"A good way to go on your last day," Stint replied.

Whuffine glanced back to see that the others had all vanished somewhere up the trail. He looked back at the three brothers. "Tell you what," he said, "you go on, tell your brother you did me in like you were told to and leave it at that."

"We don't lie to Tiny," said the one named Stint.

The third man frowned. "That's not true, Stint. Remember the porridge?"

Stint sighed. "You still on about that, Fren?"

"It had to be you!" Fren shouted.

"Listen," said the first brother, "we're wasting time and it's cold, so let's just do this, loot the shack and get on our way."

"Don't forget the hat, Gil," said Stint. "Tiny wants the hat."

Whuffine nodded. "It's a fine hat, isn't it? Alas, it's mine and I ain't selling it or giving it up."

"That's all right," said Gil, his grin broadening. "We'll take it anyway."

"You're making me defend my hat," said Whuffine, raising his walking stick and gripping the silvered end with both hands.

The three brothers laughed.

They stopped laughing when the shaft shimmered, became a thick-bladed longsword, the blade of which then burst into flames.

A rather short time later, Whuffine stood amidst sizzling chunks of human flesh, from which wisps of smoke rose as if from candlesticks. He watched the last bits of gore burn crispy black and then flake off from the blade of his sword. A moment later the weapon shimmered again and once more he was holding his walking stick. He looked down at the remnants of the three brothers and sighed. "It ain't good to get me all nostalgic."

Adjusting his fur hat, he went back inside his shack. He sat down in his captain's chair and stretched out his feet. He looked round, studying his surroundings as if seeing them for the first time. The shark-jaws lining the slatted walls, the burst of dusty, curly hairs pushing out between the boards, the lanterns and brass fittings, the casks and skinning knives and shucking stones, the harpoon heads and bundles of netting, the dhenrabi spines and Jhorlick gills, the heaps of clothing and fine cloth, and the amphorae filled with oil or wine or dyes, the clay jar on the shelf with all the gold teeth, and the half-dozen Seguleh masks . . .

Whuffine grunted. All in all, he decided, this was a far finer abode that any chilly, draught-filled temple with muttering priests for company, and all the slippy pattering of bare feet in the dead of night, as cots creaked under unusual weight and unlikely forces made them sway and jerk. Better, indeed, than the dusty shadows of the alcoves smeared in old wax and crowded with pointless offerings, where spiders built webs only to die of starvation and their tiny shriveled bodies crunched down to bitter nothing between the teeth.

But somewhere in that temple, it was held, there was faith, thick as curdled cream, upon which a god could grow fat. Well, he'd yet to see that happen. The corridors echoed with pointless hopes and muddled ambitions, with sordid crimes and petty betrayals. Faith was a claw hammer to pry loose the boards beneath the commonry's feet, an executioner's axe to lop off the heads of unbelievers, a flaring torch to set light to the kindling crowding a thrashing fool bound to a stake. Whuffine snorted. Why, a god could get sick with this lot, no doubt about it.

If it wasn't too much work, he would have ended this world long ago, and without much regret.

But I'll settle for what washes up every morning. The bodies and dead dreams, the brave and the insipid, the frightened and the belligerent, the wise ones—but oh how rare they are!—and the idiots, of which there are far too many.

"Ah, listen to me, all nostalgic again."

Slithering with all the stealth she could muster, Witch Hurl moved among the chopped-up hunks of scorched meat outside the door to Whuffine's shack. She gathered a few clumps up and under one arm and continued on up the trail.

This meat was fresh. This meat wouldn't sour her stomach the way that dead man had, and she wouldn't have to listen to any endless nattering about crossing the ocean and getting home, when all he had left was his head, or his cry of thanks when she kicked it into the waves.

She tore off mouthfuls of the human flesh, swallowing without chewing.

Remembering everything gave her good reasons, now, reasons to continue on, up into the village, where she would deliver a night of vengeful mayhem that, by dawn, would see not a single villager left alive.

And you, Feloovil Generous, you I'll save for the last. You betrayed me when I needed you the most, and for that you will pay—by all the hoary pig-gods of the Hog Harbingers of Blearmouth—may their bones rot in their stupid little barrows—you will pay, aye, Feloovil.

Because, woman, I remember everything!

With every mouthful of bloody flesh she swallowed, she felt her strength returning.

Soon, everyone dies! She cackled, choked, and then spat out a sliver of shattered thighbone.

Behind her, the storm struck the shore, and its howl filled the air. Reaching the rise and coming in sight of Spendrugle, Witch Hurl paused. A single glaring light was visible in the distant keep tower. *My tower! My keep!*

Such a delicious night of slaughter awaited them all!

"We take the beach trail," said Ackle, "but then cut off from it while still on the rise. Then it's two hundred paces along the goat trail further down the coast. There's a cut that leads down to a secluded strip of sand."

"If you say so," Spilgit said. He was freezing, clutching his shovel in hands swiftly growing numb. The light was almost gone, the wind turning ferocious and it buffeted them as they trudged along. Keeping his head down

The Wurms of Blearmouth

against the sea spray slanting in almost horizontal, Spilgit stayed a step behind Ackle.

They were halfway along the coast trail when Spilgit heard the man grunt and saw him stagger to one side.

A wild-haired old woman was suddenly before him, shrieking and lunging with hands hooked like talons.

Spilgit swung the shovel and the clang when the flat of the blade struck the woman's forehead was like a hammer on an anvil. The impact sent her tumbling into the brush between the trail and the beach.

"Gods below! Who was that?"

Ackle reappeared and joined Spilgit as they peered into the tangled thicket. "Did you kill her?"

Spilgit licked his lips, his heart pounding hard in his chest. "I don't know. She attacked me!"

"Ever seen her before?"

"No, I swear it. I thought I knew everyone."

"Maybe she came up from the sea. Another one from the wreck."

Spilgit's sigh was shaky. "I suppose so."

"You're a murderer now, Spilgit."

"No I'm not. It was an accident. It was self-defense."

"She had spindly hands and you had a shovel."

"She attacked me, you fool. You saw it."

Ackle shrugged in the gloom. "She didn't attack me. But then, I'm not a tax collector, am I?"

159

"Let's just get on with this, shall we? We're out here, might as well bring the nightmare to an end, though I'm beginning to think that end is a long way off. Don't look at me with those eyes, I'm an innocent man."

Saying nothing to that, Ackle set off once more, and Spilgit quickly followed.

Lying on the bed, Hordilo watched her getting dressed. "It's not going to happen," he said. "I mean, you were great and all, but I've had my fill of wives."

Birds Mottle glanced briefly at him before shrugging into her quilted gambeson with the huge tear exposing one breast. "Thought you never married."

"Exactly, and I mean to stay that way."

She faced him. "I was great, was I?"

"That's what I said, but don't take it to heart."

"I won't, and you know why? You weren't so great. You're so hairy I thought I was rolling with a dog."

Hordilo scowled. "I know what this is."

"What is it?"

"It's you thinking you need to throw a knife or two, since I told you I wasn't interested. Making up insults ain't no way to make yourself feel better. Maybe for a moment or two, but it never lasts. Besides, women like dogs, and I should know. So," he concluded, "it didn't work."

"Well now," said Birds, studying him, "you got all the answers, don't you?"

"I got the answers to the questions, which is better than answers to questions nobody asks, since those kind of answers are a waste of time. So, if you still got a question, ask it and I'll answer it, unless it ain't a question worth asking."

"I don't," she replied, collecting up her weapon belt. "There comes a point in a relationship when it all goes past words, or talking, even. And in the heads of the woman and the man, even thoughts dissolve into a grey, formless haze. Time itself turns into an illusion. Days and nights meld, forward and backward, up and down, now and then—all vanishing into a muddle of pointless existence." She faced him from the door. "We've reached that point, Captain."

"I ain't fooled," he said.

"By what?"

"You'll step outside the door and close it softly behind you, and lean against the wall, with tears running down your cheeks. Then you'll take a deep breath and find, from somewhere deep inside, the resolve to go on, alone, abandoned and rejected. But really, what else is there to do? The shattered, wounded heart will mend, maybe, in a decade or two. That's how it is for women and it's too bad, you know? But a man's got a thicker hide, and well, that's just natural. Something we're born with."

"How did you know?" she asked him.

He shrugged, sitting up on the bed and reaching for his trousers. "It's all there, in your pretty face."

She opened the door behind her and stepped out into the corridor. Hearing the latch drop in her wake, she made her way to the stairs. *Gods, when a woman needs a drink so soon after sex, that's a bad sign for everyone concerned.*

Reaching the top of the landing she heard a door open behind her and turned. A young woman was edging out, and there was enough about her that made it clear to Birds Mottle that this was Feloovil's daughter. Seeing Birds, the young woman hurried over. "Who are they?" she asked in a whisper.

"Always a good question," Birds replied. "Who is who?"

"Those huge men coming up the street. And one woman. Friends of yours?"

"Huge?"

"Giant!"

Birds pushed past her and hurried back up the corridor. She threw open the door to Hordilo's room. "You were right! I need you. I want you. Let's get married! Find us a shack somewhere out of the village, where we can hide away, making wild love for days on end!"

Hordilo stood, thumbs tucked into his sword belt. "A shack? Somewhere remote? Secluded, private, where no one will disturb us? Sounds like my farmhouse. Ain't been there since, well, since a while now." He smiled at her. "Who's the man with all the answers?"

"You!" she cried, rushing into his arms.

Tiny Chanter threw open the inn door and stepped forward, only to bang his head on the jamb. "Ow," he said, ducking and continuing on. Over his shoulder he said, "Lesser, Puny, fix that door, will you?"

Behind him the two brothers started hacking at the plastered beam with their axes.

"Hey!" Feloovil shouted from behind the bar. "Stop that!"

"Needs doing," Tiny said, glaring round. "Too low for a proper man, anyway."

"Then you duck!"

Tiny bared his teeth. "Tiny Chanter don't duck for nothing."

"Glad to hear it," Feloovil said, throwing a tankard at his head. It cracked hard just above his left eye, fell to a table and bounced and then dropped to the muddy floor.

"For that you die!" Tiny bellowed, one hand to his forehead.

"Before or after I serve you?" Feloovil asked.

"Make it after," said Relish, slipping past her brother. "I'm thirsty and famished!"

Flea went to a table and dragged locals from their chairs and flung them into a corner, and then he turned to his siblings. "Found us a table, Tiny!"

As Lesser and Puny, putting away their axes, hurried to join Flea, Scant and Midge, Tiny pointed a finger at Feloovil. "Ale. Food. Now."

"Pay. First."

"Tiny Chanter don't pay for nothing."

"Tiny Chanter gets hungry and thirsty, and so do his brothers and sister. Not only that," Feloovil continued, "they all get to sit outside, on the ground."

"Gods below," Relish said to Tiny, "cough up some coin, brother, so she don't spit in our bowls."

Snarling, Tiny pulled out a small pouch. He loosened the drawstrings and peered into it. He frowned, small eyes getting smaller.

Feloovil snorted, leaning her forearms on the counter. "No wonder Tiny don't pay for nothing."

Midge rose from the table and walked to the bar, shoving Relish to one side as he slapped down three silver coins.

Feloovil swept them up in one hand. "Got pretty women upstairs," she added.

"Really?" Relish asked.

•

Ackle led Spilgit down to a shelf of sand and crushed shells well back from the thundering surf, but spray engulfed them nonetheless, icy and fierce. Lightning flashed through the massive storm cloud roiling above the wild seas, thunder drumming through the howl of the wind, and Ackle was hunched over like an old man, prodding the ground ahead every now and then with his shovel. At last he halted and faced Spilgit. "Here," he said.

"Then start digging," Spilgit replied.

"I'm freezing."

"The exercise will fix that."

"No, I mean I'm freezing solid. My arms barely bend. I can't straighten my legs. There's ice in my eyes and my tongue feels like frozen leather."

Spilgit scowled. "Stop pretending to be dead, damn you! You think I'm not cold? Gods below, go on, then. Freeze solid for all I care." Pushing Ackle back, he set to digging in the heavy, ice-laden sand. "If this is a waste of time," he said in a snarl, "you're not leaving this spot, Ackle. In fact, I'm digging you a grave, right here."

"It's there, Spilgit. My haul. My hoard. Enough to buy a damned estate, maybe two, if one of them is run-down and occupied by an old woman who's half mad and eats bats for breakfast. The kind of woman you can push down the stairs and no servants to ask any questions, so the property just falls into your lap, because of debts or whatnot—"

"What in Hood's name are you going on about?" Spilgit demanded, glaring up at the man. "What old woman? What debts?"

"I'm just saying. I was the last one to go, you see, and maybe bats were fine with her but I was down to making tea from cobwebs, and yet I stayed on as long as I could, and did I get a word of thanks? Not on your life. That hag spat on me and clawed my face, but the candlesticks were my severance pay—she promised them to me! Instead, she rips the pack and everything falls out, and then she kicks my shin and tries to sink her teeth in my throat. But she didn't have any teeth. She gummed my neck, Spilgit, and that wasn't a pleasant experience."

Spilgit laughed harshly. "You ran from an old woman. Gods, Ackle, you really are pathetic."

"She probably poisoned me. Or cursed me. Or both. I

was actually looking forward to a proper death, you know. Just an end to this whole miserable existence. I'd earned it, in fact—"

Something clunked under Spilgit's shovel. Breathing hard from the exertion, Spilgit worked the blade around the object, and moments later he could make out the curved lid of a banded chest.

"That's it," said Ackle. "I told you I wasn't lying."

Spilgit set the shovel aside and pulled at the chest, working it free. It was heavy and he grunted lifting it from the hole. "Hold on," he said, eyes finding the seal over the lock, "this is a Revenue Chest!"

"That's right," said Ackle. "I beat a tax collector senseless, on the Whitter Road just east of Elin. With a candlestick."

"You stole tax revenue!"

"Just getting my own back, Spilgit. Anyway, you quit as a tax collector, so what difference does it make to you? You're getting half, besides."

Spilgit climbed out of the hole, brushed sand from his hands, and then leapt at Ackle. "Thief!" His hands closed on the man's twisted, scarred neck, and his weight drove Ackle down to the ground. Spilgit knelt on him, squeezing with all his strength, seeing the ugly eyes bulge, the deepening hue of the face going from blue to grey. "This time you die for real! Just what you wanted!"

Ackle's struggles fell away, his kicking stilled, and all life vanished from his mottled face.

Still Spilgit gripped Ackle's throat, gasping out the last of his rage. "Thief," he said again, but this time without much feeling. "Look at you. Got your wish, fool. This was punishment. Legal execution, in fact. I'm still a tax collector—it's in my blood, in my bones, gods, in my hands!" He pulled his grip free, crawled off the corpse.

Eyes falling to the chest, he frowned. "Stolen revenues. For building better roads. Lanterns in the streets. Keeping the drains clear. But still, well, a man needs to get properly set up. It's not like they'll take me back, anyway. I could go into accountancy, use my skills for the other side. A nice office, in a decent neighbourhood, in a fine city, with proper clothes. Servants. It's what I deserve, after a year in Spendrugle. Year? Only a year? More like a century!" Reaching over he pulled close the chest, broke the seal and flipped back the lid.

The coins were properly columned, each column wrapped and sealed and marked with the total amount. They'd already been converted, meaning every damned coin was solid gold. *This wasn't no normal haul. Not some scrapings from villages, farms and hamlets. Gods below, this was a city's take. What in Hood's name was that tax collector doing with it on Whitter Road? Without an armed escort?*

Spilgit, you fool, the bastard was stealing it, of course!

He dropped the lid. He was getting cold again, now that he'd stopped digging and strangling Ackle. He had enough coin here to buy Spendrugle, all the lands surrounding it, and that damned Wurms Keep. He had the coin to hire an army and march back in the summer and lay waste to the whole place, and it was only what they all deserved.

Spilgit stood, staring down at the chest.

The shovel flattened the back of his skull and he toppled forward. His legs kicked a few times then went straight as spears. Ackle studied the sprawled corpse of the tax collector. "I told you I was dead!" he shouted. "You can't kill a dead man! I told you!"

Dropping the shovel, he fell to his knees and pushed the chest back into the hole. It could all wait until the spring, anyway. Too cold for travel. His joints were freezing solid, making every move a creaking ordeal.

Ackle filled in the hole again, and then took up Spilgit by the ankles and dragged him to the edge of the shelf. He kicked the body into the thrashing surf, watched as the corpse was tugged out to sea, sucked down and out of sight between two massive rocks.

"Killing tax collectors," he muttered. "I could make a living out of that."

Picking up both shovels, he set off for the village.

. . .

Witch Hurl crawled up from the bushes and made it onto the trail on her hands and knees. Blood dripped sluggishly from her forehead, but the cold had frozen most of it. She had to hand it to Spilgit: the man's reflexes were like lightning. Still, no matter. Against nine of her, he would have no chance, and indeed the time had come.

Muttering under her breath, she sembled. Her form blurred, she yowled in pain, and moments later nine lizard cats emerged from the redolent, spicy haze. The wind whipped those scents away. Her bodies were scrawny, but filled with venomous hatred. She slipped forward, tails writhing, nine slinky forms rushing up the trail.

The King's Heel. It would all start there, with the conclusion of plenty of unfinished business. It was likely all the denizens of the village were in there, anyway, meaning she wouldn't have to do much hunting through houses and huts, pigsties and stables. No, they would all be crowded in the Heel tonight, sitting out the storm, warm in each other's stink.

She would make of that wretched inn a tomb, a haunted crypt, its walls sweating the blood of slaughter, the echoes running in all directions from the screams and shrieks and death rattles.

Racing closer, her gazes caught once more the glaring light from the tower of Wurms Keep. Her fury sizzled like fat in a pan, and she found her throats opening to hisses and then spitting, every scale upon her nine backs arching into serrated lines.

There, directly ahead, the entrance to the King's Heel. Reaching it, she flung herselves against the barrier. And rebounded. Frustrated rage filled her bodies. Claws were unsheathed, lashing out at the wind, gouging deep furrows in the frozen mud. She glared at the door, willing it to explode. But it defied her power. Hurl screamed through nine throats.

At the high-pitched wailing from outside, Feloovil shivered. "The wind's gone mad out there! Here, then, have another drink!"

Laughing, Relish held up her tankard, watching it weave before her. "Brilliant idea," she shouted. "A tavern on a ship! We should've thought of that years ago!"

"You ain't on a ship no more," Tiny said, his small red eyes tracking the room before returning to their concentrated fixation on Feloovil's breasts. "You're drunk," he explained. "That's why you're all wavering back and forth, and the floor keeps tilting, and those lanterns swaying like that." He belched then and leaned on the counter to get closer to those breasts, and then he addressed them. "I know you're old and all," he said, with a bleary smile, "but that just makes you more desperate, and a desperate woman is my kind of woman."

"The only kind, I would think," Feloovil replied. "And I'll have you know I'm only thirty-one years old."

"Hah hah hah!"

"Now, if you had me some offerings," she continued, ignoring his derision, "I might show you the youth of my soul and all that."

"Oh," Tiny replied, "I'll offer you something all right. Hah hah hah!"

"Listen to that wind!" Relish said, swinging round to face the door. "Like voices! Screaming witches! Ugly hags riding the black winds!" She looked round, frowned at all the pale faces and the huddling forms at the tables. "Wind's got you all terrified! You're all useless, the worst sailors I ever seen. All hands on deck! Storm-sails, reef the jibe and trim the anchor!" She spun back to Feloovil. "I want some women!"

"She can do that," Tiny said, nodding, "since it keeps her a virgin, and we promised old Ma we'd keep her virtue and dignity and stuff."

Feloovil shrugged. "Head on up and find one, then," she said to Relish.

Weaving, Relish made her way to the stairs.

Feloovil eyed Tiny Chanter. "You got small hands," she said.

"They ain't small."

"Too small for the rest of you, I mean. That's not too promising."

"Tiny don't make promises," he replied, nodding at her breasts. "Tiny Chanter does whatever he wants to do, with anybody he wants to do them with, as long as they do what they're told, they'll do fine."

"They'll do fine all right," Feloovil said. "And I bet you want to see them naked, don't you?"

He smiled.

"All right, then," she said. "Here's the deal. You all look tough and that's good. There's someone up at the keep needs killing."

"I can kill," Tiny said. "Better than anybody. Just ask 'em, all those people I killed. I ain't just a sword, neither. I got sorcery. Necromancy. Jhistal, Demidrek, High Mage. Pick a title, I'm it."

"Even better," she said. "Since that keep's full of sorcerers right now. Lord Fangatooth Claw, and his guests. Bauchelain and Korbal Broach."

Tiny seemed to reel for a moment, and then his face darkened. "Aye, them. Wait, who's Lord Fangatooth Claw?"

"The local tyrant," she replied.

Tiny grunted. "Nice name."

"He thinks so," said Feloovil. "So, that's the deal." She lifted her breasts. "You get these, in all their glory. But you got to kill everyone in that keep first."

"We can do that," Tiny said. "We was going to do it anyway."

"Oh. Well, then—"

"After we killed all of you," Tiny went on. "But instead, we'll do it the other way round. Keep first and then everybody here, but not till after you and me do . . . you know . . . the stuff men and women do. The pinky stuff."

"The what?"

Tiny reddened. "Pinky naked, I mean. You know."

"You ain't never done any of that before, have you?"

"Of course I have!"

But Feloovil shook her head. "If you had, you'd know that what your sister's doing upstairs with one of my girls makes her no virgin in anyone's eyes."

"Watch your mouth!" he snarled, reaching for his sword.

"Never mind what I just said, Tiny. Go on and kill them up there, if you think you can. Wurms Keep."

"We will! And then we come back down and kill all of you!"

"The walk will sober you up, I hope," she said, glancing over at Tiny's equally drunk brothers. "You'll need your wits about you."

"Tiny don't need no wits about him," Tiny replied.

"You're giving me all the reasons I need know about why you're called Tiny," said Feloovil. "But I'm sure I'll get a few more by the time we're done."

He jabbed a finger at her. "Count on it!" Turning to his brothers he said, "On your feet all of you! It's time! In the keep up there, we'll find Lord Fungaltooth and those two from the *Suncurl*!"

"Who's Lord Fingaltooth?" Midge asked.

"A dead man!" shouted Tiny.

Flea frowned and said, "We gonna kill a dead man, Tiny? What for?"

"No, he ain't dead yet, Flea. But he's going to be, when he meets us!"

Midge laughed. "And he won't be no Lord Fancytooth then, will he? Ha ha!"

"Fumbletooth," corrected Tiny.

Feloovil watched the huge man draw his equally huge sword, and felt a brief wilting of anticipation. Shaking it off, she pointed at the door. "On your way, Chanters. Destiny awaits!"

"Ha ha ha," said Midge. "Destiny's taking us up to the keep! Where is she, then?"

"Get the door, Puny," commanded Tiny. "We'll re-group in the street, and then begin our charge on the keep walls."

"Up that hill?" Lesser asked.

"Tiny don't do hills," Tiny said in a growl. "We charge and that's that. We take the walls, and then we slaughter everyone!"

"Hey," said Puny, "where's Stint and Gil and Fren?"

"Probably ran off with your new hat, Tiny," said Scant.

"We'll deal with them later," Tiny snapped.

Puny walked to the door and swung it open.

"As far as stupid ideas go," whispered Sordid, "this is our worst one yet." She was crouched with the rest of the squad, barring Birds Mottle, in the ditch beside the track, not thirty paces from the keep's gatehouse. From their hidden vantage point, they studied the lone guard stand-ing in front of that gate.

"You got a bad attitude there, Sordid," said Bisk Fatter in low tones. "It's always been your problem, you know. You're always wanting to stand apart from the rest of us, as if you were special or something. Smarter, maybe."

"Prettier, that's for sure," Heck Urse said.

"Shut your mouth, Heck," said Bisk in a growl. "Listen, Sordid, it's bad for morale."

She turned to study the man. "Morale? Have you lost your mind, sir?"

"We can do this," said Bisk, glowering in the gloom. "He's just one guard, for Hood's sake."

"But he'th juth sthanding there," hissed Gust Hubb. "Thorm'th howling and wind'th blowing and thill he juth sthans there, holding tha' sthworth."

Sordid saw Wormlick slide close to Gust, reach up with one gloved fist, and knock on the side of the man's head.

Gust flinched away. "I ain't thimple, you fool. Juth got a sthliced thongue."

"And one eye, no nose and no ears, and bite marks on your legs." Wormlick laughed.

"Sthooth thoo clothe to Manthy, ith all."

"Gave you the title, I'd say," Wormlick went on. "Gust Hubb the Luckless. Sorry. The Luckleth." He sniggered.

"Look whothe thalking, you pock-faced hog-butt."

"Keep it down you two!" Bisk commanded in a rasp. "Someone throw a rock against the wall. Make the guard turn round, and then we rush him."

Sordid faced the guard again and shook her head. "He ain't right, sir. Too pale. Too bloated."

Heck Urse pushed up beside her, squinting. "Necromancy! That's man's dead. That's one of our shipmates from the *Suncurl*. That's Briv, who drowned."

Gust Hubb joined them on the bank. "Briv the carpenter's helper or Briv the rope maker?"

"That don't matter," whispered Heck. "This is Korbal Broach's work."

"So what?" Bisk said behind them. "Dead or alive, it's just one man." He pulled up a stone from the ditch. "Get ready." He straightened slowly, and then threw the stone. It sailed over the guard's head and thumped high on the wooden gate.

The guard turned.

"Now!"

The squad rose from the ditch and rushed forward.

But somehow, still the guard faced them, and was now raising his sword.

The charge slowed, wavered.

"How did he do that?" Wormlick demanded.

"It's not the same man!" Heck said. "That's Briv one of the other ones!"

"He thowed them thogether!" shrieked Gust Hubb.

The squad's charge dribbled away, and they stood staring at the new guard, with fifteen paces between them.

The dead man lifted his sword with some alacrity.

"A guard no one can sneak up behind!" cried Heck Urse.

"Gods below," said Sordid. "That's the stupidest thing I have ever seen."

"You're only saying that," retorted Heck, "because you weren't on the *Suncurl!*"

"Wormlick, you and Bisk go to the right. Heck and Gust, to the left. Follow me." She headed forward, drawing her fighting knives.

"I'm corporal here, Sordid—"

"Just follow, sir."

The others fanned out while Sordid advanced on the guard. "Hey!" she shouted.

As she suspected, the guard facing the gate sought to turn round. The other one resisted the effort and they stumbled.

Bisk howled and charged in from one side, trailed by Wormlick, while Heck attacked from the opposite flank. Gust Hubb stumbled on something and fell hard on the track. He cried out as he landed on his shortsword.

The guard tottered about, waving swords that kept clashing against one another.

Sordid came in low and hamstrung the creature. It fell over, just as Bisk shrieked and swung his huge two-handed sword. The heavy blade swished over the guard and flew from the corporal's hands. It sailed across the track and speared Gust Hubb through the right thigh. He loosed another howl.

Heck Urse reached the fallen guard and hacked at both heads. "Briv and Briv! Die! Die and die and die again!"

Sordid backed away. "Wormlick, check on Gust. See how bad it is."

Wormlick laughed. "How bad? The fool's skewered through the leg! And he fell on his sword! He's spurting blood everywhere!"

"Then bandage him up, damn you!"

"You ain't corporal—"

"No," she snapped. "Our corporal's the one who speared him! I'm busting him down right now. Whose plan was this? Did it work? Of course it worked. Why? Because it was my plan! Listen, all of you, I'm now Captain."

"Sergeant, shouldn't it be?" Heck asked, still gasping from hacking open Briv and Briv's heads.

"Captain! Sater always had it in mind to promote me."

"Since when?" Bisk demanded.

"Since I just said so."

Gust's howls went on and on.

At that moment the gate swung open and there stood a tall man with a forked beard. "Ah," he said, eyes alighting upon Gust Hubb, "the late Captain Sater's redoubtable soldiers . . . and friends. Well, your timing is impeccable. I have just made cookies."

Emancipor Reese sat across from Korbal Broach, watching the huge, fat man licking the icing from one of Bauchelain's creations. His stomach rumbled and then gurgled. "How is it you're allowed to eat them, then," he asked.

Korbal blinked at him, said nothing.

There was a commotion from one end of the dining hall and a moment later, amidst clumping boots, gasps, whispers and moans, Bauchelain returned leading a woman and three men carrying between them a fourth, who had a massive sword thrust through one thigh, and a short sword driven up into an armpit. His bandaged form was splashed with blood.

Emancipor pointed a finger at one of the men helping this unfortunate comrade to a nearby bench. "You was on the *Suncurl*," he said. "You led the charge onto the Chanters' ship during the mating and the battle and all. Then you stole one of their lifeboats and lit out."

The man glared. "Aye, Mancy. I'm Heck Urse. And this is the rest of Sater's squad. They chased us down, all the way from Stratem."

"Very loyal of them," said Bauchelain, resuming his

---

seat. "Korbal, my friend, will you do me a favour? This poor wounded man needs healing."

At that the bandaged man suddenly sat up. "No!" he cried. "I'm bether!"

Korbal set the cookie—stripped clean of its covering of icing—down on the table, and then rose and walked over to the wounded man, who shrank back. When Korbal tugged the sword from the thigh, the man swooned, which made removing the shorter sword much simpler. Weapons clanging to the floor, Korbal Broach began peeling sodden bandages from the man.

Emancipor could see that this effort was going to take some time. He rose and reached out across the table for the cookie Korbal had left behind, only to have his hand slapped by Bauchelain.

"Now now, Mister Reese, what did I tell you?" Bauchelain then gingerly picked up the lone cookie, and slipped it into a pocket beneath his cloak, but not before Emancipor caught a glimpse of the pattern incised on the top of the flat cookie.

From somewhere below came a long, wavering scream.

The squad soldiers started.

"That would be our host," Bauchelain said, smiling. "I believe he is torturing prisoners in the cells below. However, I am assured he will be joining us soon, to partake of my baking."

"He'll want a food tester," Emancipor predicted, set-
tling back and reaching for his goblet of wine.

"I sincerely doubt that," Bauchelain replied. "Lord
Fangatooth is doomed to bravado, as we shall soon see.
In any case, I shall be his food tester."

"But with you immune to poisons, Master—"

"I assure you, Mister Reese, no poison is involved."

"So how come the fancy patterns beneath the icing,
Master?"

"My private signature, Mister Reese, that shall remain
so, yes? Now, although I am not yet the host, permit me,
if you will, to be mother." Bauchelain gestured with one
thin, pale hand to the plate heaped with cookies. "Do
help yourselves, will you?"

The woman snorted and said, "Wine will do for us,
thank you. No, Heck, don't be a fool. Just wine."

Bauchelain shrugged. "As you wish. Of course, a lesser
man than I would be offended, given my efforts in the
kitchen and whatnot."

"That's too bad," the woman replied with all the sincer-
ity of a banker. "Heck was telling us about compensation.
For injuries and all. Also, there's the whole matter of our
cut in the haul from Toll's City, which Sater promised us."

"Ah," murmured Bauchelain, nodding as he sipped his
wine, "of course. It would be coin, wouldn't it, behind
your impressive, if somewhat unreasonable, pursuit across

an entire ocean. We are indeed driven to our baser natures in this instinctive hunger for . . . well, for what, precisely? Security? Stability? Material possessions? Status? All of these, surely, in varying measures. If a dog understood gold and silver, why, I am sure the beast would be no different from anyone here. Excepting me and Korbal Broach, of course, for whom wealth is but a means to an end, not to mention cogently regarded with wisdom, with respect to its ephemeral presumption of value." He smiled at the woman and raised his goblet. "Coin and theft, then, shall we call them bedmates? Two sides of the same wretched piece of metal? Or does greed stand alone, and find in gold and silver nothing but pretty symbols of its inherent venality? Do we hoard by nature? Do we invest against the unknown and unknowable future, and in stacks of coin seek to amend the fates? We would make of our lives a soft, cushioned bed, warm and eternal, and see a fine end—if we must—shrouded in the selfsame sheets. Oh, well."

The woman turned to Emancipor. "Does he always go on like this?" Without awaiting an answer she faced Bauchelain again. "Anyway, cough up our share of the coin and we'll be on our way."

"Alas," said Bauchelain, "we do not possess it. I imagine the bulk of the treasure will be found beneath the wreck of the *Suncurl*. That said, you are welcome to it all."

Emancipor grunted. "If that comber ain't collected it already."

"Oh, I doubt that, Mister Reese, given the inclement weather. But the townsfolk, being wreckers, will of course contest any claim to that treasure."

Sordid snorted. "That's fine. Let them try."

Bauchelain studied her for a moment, and then said, "I am afraid you do not intrigue me in the least, which is unfortunate, as you are rather attractive, but by your tone and the cast of your face, I see both inclined to dissolution in the near future. How sad."

She glared at him, and then slouched back in her chair, drew a knife and began paring her nails. "Now it's insults, is it?"

"Forgive me," said Bauchelain, "if in expressing my disinterest you find yourself feeling diminished."

"Not nearly as diminished as you'll feel with a slit throat."

"Oh dear, we descend to threats."

Korbal Broach returned to the table, sat and looked round for his cookie. Frowning, he reached out for another one.

"My friend," said Bauchelain, "I ask that you refrain for the moment."

"But I like icing, Bauchelain. I like it. I want it."

"The bowl awaits you in the kitchen, since I instructed

Mister Reese to make twice as much as needed, knowing as I do your inclinations. Is that not so, Mister Reese?"

"Oh aye, Master, half a bowl in the kitchen. Ground powder of sugar cane, moderately bleached and with a touch of honey, too. Nice and cool by now, I should think."

Smiling, Korbal Broach rose and left the dining hall.

Emancipor looked over at the bench to see that Heck had gone over to his companion, who was now sitting up. Divested of bandages, he was now recognizable as Gust Hubb, although one of his eyes was green while the other was grey, sporting a new pink nose that was decidedly feminine, and the ears were mismatched as well, but of scars and wounds there was no sign.

"High Denul!" hissed Heck Urse, shaking his friend by the shoulder. "You're all healed, Gust! You look perf—as handsome as ever!"

"I'm marked," groaned Gust. "He marked me. Might as well be dead!"

"But you're not! You're healed!"

Gust looked up, wiped at his eyes and sniffled. "Where's Birds? I want Birds to see me."

"She will, Gust. Better yet, we're getting our cut! All we got to do is kill all the wreckers and go out to the *Suncurl* and collect it all up!"

"Really?"

"Really! See, it's all worked out for the best!"

Gust slowly smiled.

A moment later Lord Fangatooth Claw strode into the room, drying his hands with a small towel, and in his wake trailed Scribe Coingood, pale and sweaty and, as usual, burdened with wood-framed wax tablets. Eyes alighting on the heap of cookies on the pewter plate in the centre of the table, the lord nodded. "My, don't those look tasty!"

"Oh they are," said Bauchelain, reaching out without looking and taking one. He bit it in half, chewed and swallowed, and then plopped the second half into his mouth and followed that down with some wine. Sighing, he settled back. "Delicious, but of course that does not surprise me. I speak not from a dearth of modesty, as the kitchen was impressively stocked, Lord Fangatooth. Most impressively."

"It is nonetheless a shame," said Fangatooth, "that the sacred notion of host and guest must be dispensed with before the dawn."

"I fully understand," said Bauchelain. "After all, we are two sorcerers under the same roof. High Mages, in fact, and so see in each other the deadliest of rivals. Like two male wolves in their prime, with but one pack awaiting the victor."

"Just so," Fangatooth said, pouring himself some

wine—all the servants were gone, it seemed, or perhaps in hiding. The lord lifted the goblet and then made rolling motions with his other hand. "Rivals indeed. Tyrants in the same bed. Rather, the blanket, only big enough to warm one of us. While in that bed. Two fish in the same basin, and only one rock to hide under." He faltered for a moment, and then said, "Oh yes, just as I said, Bauchelain. Rivals, in the midst of deadly rivalry. Foes, already locked in a contest of powers, and wits." Then he blinked and looked round. "Why, it seems we shall have ourselves an audience as well! Excellent. Dear strangers, make yourselves at home as my guests!"

"Right," said the woman in a drawl, "at least until you decide to kill us."

"Precisely."

She faced Bauchelain. "Whereas you are prepared to let us go, is that right?"

"Why, so it is."

"All right, then, we're with you, and not just for that, but for healing Gust, too."

Smiling at her, Bauchelain said, "Why, you grow warmer in my eyes, my dear."

"Keep it up," she said, "and I might melt."

"You do understand, don't you," said Bauchelain, "that I see little of the negative in dissolution?"

She grunted. "Why, that makes two of us. Which is

why you're too upright for me. Sorry, but we won't be rolling in a wedding bed anytime soon, I'm afraid."

"Hence my earlier sadness."

Fangatooth cleared his throat, rather loudly. "I see, Bauchelain, that you have commandeered my chair at the head of the table."

"My apologies, sir. An oversight. Or, perhaps, impatience?"

"No matter. In any case, you will not leave this room alive, I'm afraid. I have sealed the chamber in the deadliest of wards. Death awaits you at every exit. I note, of course, that your friend, the eunuch, is not here. But so too is the kitchen sealed, and should he endeavour to return here, intending to assist you once he hears your terrible cries, he will die a most terrible death."

Bauchelain reached for another cookie. Bit, chewed and swallowed.

"The sorcery I have perfected," Fangatooth continued, "is solely devoted to the necessities of tyranny. The delivery of pain, the evocation of horror, the agony of agony—Scribe!"

"Milord?"

"Are you writing all this down?"

"I am, milord."

"My last line, get rid of it. Devise something better."

"At once, milord."

Emancipor filled up his pipe and lit it using one of the candles on the table. He drew deeply and filled his lungs with smoke, and then frowned. "Oh no," he said. "Wrong blend." The scene sagged before his eyes. *Oh, and that was uncut, too.* His eyes fixed on the plate of cookies. Sweat sprang out under his clothes. He could feel his heart palpitating, and saliva drenched his mouth.

As Bauchelain reached for a third cookie, Fangatooth held up a hand and said, "Please, you have well made your point, Bauchelain! I know well that these cookies are no more than a distraction, a feint, a not-so-clever attempt at misdirection! No, I imagine you have secreted about you an ensorcelled sword, or knife, as you clearly appraise yourself a warrior of some sort. But I am afraid to say, such things only bore me." He reached out and collected up a cookie. Examined it a moment, and then used one fingernail to scratch loose some icing, which he then brought to his mouth, and tasted. "Ah, very nice." He bit the cookie in half, chewed and swallowed, and bit the next piece in half, and then the next, and so on until the cookie was gone, except for a single crumb on one finger, which he ate whole.

He sat back and smiled across at Bauchelain. "Now, shall we begin?"

Bauchelain's brows lifted. "Begin? Why, sir, it is already over."

"What do you mean?"

"I mean that I have won, Lord Fangatooth."

The man leapt upright. "It was poisoned! A double blind deception! Oh you fool, think you I am not also immune to all poisons?"

"I am sure that you are," Bauchelain replied. "But that will not avail you, alas."

"Prepare to defend yourself!"

Bauchelain sipped at his wine.

Emancipor, trembling to keep from stealing a cookie, started as Fangatooth suddenly clutched his stomach and gasped.

"What? What have you done to me?"

"Why," said Bauchelain, "I have killed you."

The lord staggered back, doubling over in pain. He shrieked. Then blood erupted from him, spraying out from his body. He straightened, arching as if taken by spasms, and his torso bulged horribly, only to then split open.

The demon that crawled out of Fangatooth's body was as big as a man. It had four arms and two bent, ape-like legs with talons on the end of its toes. Beneath a low, hairless pate, its face was broad and dominated by a mouth bristling with needlelike fangs. Smeared in gore, it clambered free of Fangatooth's ruptured corpse, and then coughed and spat.

Lifting its ghastly head, the demon glared at Bauchelain, and then spoke in a rasping, reptilian voice, "That was a dirty trick!"

Bauchelain shrugged. "Hardly," he said. "Well, perhaps, somewhat unkind. In any case, you will be relieved to know that I am done with you, and so you may now return to Aral Gamelain, with my regards to your Lord."

The demon showed its fangs in a bristling grimace or grin, and then vanished.

"Mister Reese!"

Bauchelain's hand slashed down, knocking the cookie only a hair's breadth from Emancipor's mouth.

"Beneath the icing, my friend, you will find pentagrams of summoning! Ones in which the demon so summoned is already bound by me, until such time that the pattern is broken by someone else! Now, step back, Mister Reese, at once. You were one cookie away from death, and I'll not warn you again!"

"I was just going to lick off the icing, Master—"

"You were not! And that is not rustleaf I am smelling from that pipe, is it?"

"My apologies, Master. It didn't occur to me to think."

"Yes," Bauchelain replied, eyeing him, "upon that we are agreed."

The dissolute woman stood. "Glad that's all over with, then," she said. "Lord Bauchelain, would you be so kind as to disperse all those deadly wards surrounding this chamber?"

Bauchelain waved a hand. "Korbal did so already, my dear. But will you not stay the rest of the night?"

She turned to her squadmates. "Find beds, soldiers. A dry and warm night until we greet the new dawn!"

At that moment a loud crashing sound came from the stairs. Blearily, Emancipor turned to the doorway beyond which was the wide hallway that led to the staircase in time to see that door burst apart in splinters and shards, with a dented, broken golem tumbling into the chamber. Its bucket head rolled away from its leaking body, rocked back and forth for a moment and then fell still.

From somewhere atop the stairs came Korbal Broach's high, piping voice. "It was an accident!"

Yowling in frenzy, Witch Hurl fought among herselves just outside the door to the King's Heel. She cursed that infernal barrier, and the pathetic claw-clattering paws sadly lacking in thumbs, a detail that made the door stand triumphant and mocking before her glaring, raging eyes.

The wind buffeted her writhing, spitting forms, forcing a few of her to slink low upon the frozen mud of the street. And still the fury within her burgeoned. Her serrated

scales running the length of her spines were almost verti-
cal; her tails whipped and reared like seaworms awaiting a
fast-descending corpse. Her jaws stretched wide to lock
the hinges of her canines, and that horrible wind whipped
into the cavern of her mouths, cold and lifeless but hungry all the same. She slashed the ground with her claws.
She leapt into the air in berserk rage, only to be flung
sideways by the gusts storming down the street.

Murder filled her mind, a word that stood alone, that
floated and surged up and down and slid to one side only
to swim back to the centre of her thoughts. She could
taste that word, its sweet roundness, it slithering tail of
sound at the end of its utterance that stung like tart berries in a goat's belly. Fires licked around it, smoke curled
from it, blackening the air. It was a word with a thousand
faces and a thousand expressions displaying but the faintest variations of universal dismay.

She wanted to eat that word. Take it by the neck and
hold on until all life left it. She wanted to leap upon it
after a vicious rush low over the ground. She wanted to
eye it venomously, unblinkingly, from nearby cover. She
wanted it to stalk her dreams.

And in the midst of this mental tantrum of desire, the
cruel door buckled, indifference torn away until its very
bones of flat wood and banded bronze quivered as if with
ague, and then it swung open.

Witch Hurl converged upon that misshapen eruption of light, and the figure silhouetted within it.

Murder!

Puny bellowed and staggered back. Scaly creatures clung to him, upon his chest, fighting to close jaws on his throat; upon his arms where they writhed like tentacles; another attempting to burrow into his crotch. Blood spurted. He batted at the things, tore them away, flung them in all directions.

His brothers roared. The patrons screamed.

Feloovil, standing behind the bar, hissed a vile curse under her breath.

Nine lizard cats and not one of them much bigger than a house cat, or a scrawny, worm-ridden barn mouser. But this did nothing to mitigate their viciousness.

Puny clambered back onto his feet. Tiny and the others began swinging their huge weapons. Blades crashed through chairs, tables. Shrieks ended in frothy gurgles as those weapons struck hapless locals. Severed skull-pates knotted with hair spun across the room; limbs flopped, bounced and twitched atop tables or on the muddy and now bloody floor. The lizard cats evaded every blow, spinning, leaping, darting, clawing at everyone.

Feloovil beheld utter carnage from her place behind the bar. She saw two of the brothers struggling to ready a three-handed sword, only to wither to an exploding table-top, staggering apart, their faces and necks studded with splinters. A cat leapt to wrap itself around the side of one of the brother's heads, tearing the ear off with its jaws, while the other brother stumbled over a chair that collapsed under him, and as he thumped on the floor, four cats closed in. His scream became a spray.

Then, as if of one mind, the lizard cats spied Feloovil, and all nine suddenly rushed her, leaping over the counter. Their multiple impacts made her stagger back. She screamed as talons raked through her tunic, bit deep into her flesh. Clothes disintegrating under the assault, she was stripped naked in a welter of blood.

Until one cat, seeking to sink its fangs into one of her breasts, instead found savage teeth clamping about its throat. A moment later another cat howled as another mouth, this one from the other breast, caught hold of one of his forelimbs and bit down hard enough to break bones.

All at once, more mouths appeared upon Feloovil's ample form: upon her shoulders; upon her low-slung belly; her thighs. Another split open on her forehead. Each one stretched wide, bearing teeth sharp as knifepoints.

"You damned witch!" Feloovil shrieked from countless mouths. "Get away from me! I am your goddess, you stupid fool!"

In the room before Feloovil and her snarling or yowling attackers, where only a few huddled figures still twitched amidst the wreckage, and only three of the Chanter brothers stood with heaving chests, with weapons draining blood and gore, with lacerations upon their bodies, faces turned, eyes fixed upon the battle on the other side of the bar.

A dead cat, its throat crushed and leaking, hung from Feloovil's left breast. The cat trapped by the other breast's mouth had clawed that swelling of soft flesh into ragged ribbons, and still the mouth held on, masticating to grind through the creature's forelimb.

The other cats withdrew, crowded on the blood-smeared countertop, and then from their throats came a wavering, shrill chorus of voices. *"She's mine! You promised! Your daughter is mine! Her blood! Her everything!"*

"Never!" Feloovil screamed.

Its ruined limb chewed through, the cat upon her right breast fell away, running three sets of claws down Feloovil's belly on its way to the floor. She glanced down and stamped on its head, making a crushed-egg sound.

The remaining cats all flinched, barring the dead one hanging from the other breast.

Feloovil's many mouths all grinned most evilly. "I got rid of you once, Hurl, and I'll do it again! I swear it!"

"Not you, whore! Her father did that!"

A voice then spoke from the doorway. "And it seems I shall have to do so again."

The seven remaining lizard cats all spun round. *"Whuffal Caraline Ganaggs! Vile Elder! Leave me be!"*

The grey-haired man with the finely trimmed beard, moustache and eyebrows slowly drew off his fox-fur hat. "I warned you, Witch. Now look what you've done. Nearly everyone is dead."

"Not my fault! Blame the Tarthenal!"

"Lies!" bellowed Tiny Chanter. "We was defending ourselves!"

Whuffine studied them. "Begone," he said. "I have already slain three of your siblings and if necessary, I will do away with the rest of you. It's this nostalgia," he added, with an apologetic shrug. "It's not good me getting nostalgic, you see. Not good at all."

Growling, Tiny glared about, and then said, "Tiny don't do getting killed. Let's go."

"What about Relish?" asked Midge.

Tiny pointed at Feloovil. "Send her up to the keep after us."

Feloovil's mouths twisted into sneers. "Just be glad

she ain't no virgin," those mouths all said. "Hurl wants herself a sacrifice."

"No more sacrifices," said Whuffine, leaning on his walking stick. "It's my talents with stone what's done us in here, and so it's up to me to clean all this up."

"Then kill that Fangatooth!" shrieked Feloovil.

"No need," the comber replied. "He's already dead."

"Then kill the one who killed him! Away with all sorcerers! I will not again be bound to a witch or warlock!"

Whuffine sighed. "We'll see. A word or two might be enough to send them on their way. I don't like violence. Makes me nostalgic. Makes me remember burning continents, burning skies, burning seas, mountains of the dead and all that." He pointed at the D'ivers. "Witch Hurl, best semble now."

The lizard cats drew together, blurred and then, in a slithering of spicy vapours, transformed into a scrawny hag of a woman. "Aagh!" she cried. "Look at me! My beauty, gone!"

Feloovil cackled with many of her ghastly mouths, while the others said, "You ain't worth nothing anymore, Witch. You're banished! Go on, out into the storm! And never come back!"

"Else I kill you for certain this time," added Whuffine.

"I want my keep!"

"No," said Whuffine.

"I hate you all!" Hurl hissed, rushing for the door. "Murder will have to wait. Now it's the other sweet word! Now it's hate. Hate hate hate hate! This isn't over, oh no it isn't—"

An odd sound came from the doorway, where Hurl suddenly stopped, and then stepped back, but when she did so she had no head, only an angled slice exposing her neck, from which blood pumped. Her knees then buckled and she collapsed upon the threshold.

Tiny Chanter stepped over her and peered into the tavern, looking round with a scowl. Blood trickled rivulets down the length of his huge sword's blade. "Tiny don't like witches," he said.

"Begone," Whuffine said again. "My last warning."

"We're storming the keep now," Tiny said, with a sudden bright smile.

To that, Whuffine shrugged.

"Hah hah hah!" said Tiny, before ducking back outside and bellowing commands to his brothers.

Eyes fixing on Feloovil, Whuffine sighed and shook his head. "All for a slip of the chisel," he said.

Huddled at the top of the stairs, Felittle edged back. A muffled murmuring came from between her legs, to which she responded with: "Shhh, my lovely. She won't last much longer. I promise."

And then it's my turn!

Coingood broke the last of the manacles from Warmet Humble and stepped back as the broken form sank to its knees on the stained floor. "It wasn't me," the Scribe whispered. "I'm a good scribe, honest! And I'll burn your brother's book."

Warmet slowly lifted his head and looked upon Bauchelain. "My thanks," he said. "I thought mercy was dead. I thought I would spend an eternity hanging from chains, at the whim of my foul, evil brother's lust for cruelty. His vengeance, his treachery, his brutality. See how broken I am. Perhaps I shall never heal, and so am doomed to shuffle about in these empty halls, muttering under my breath, a frail thing buffeted by inimical draughts. I see a miserable life ahead indeed, but I bless you nonetheless. Freedom never tasted as sweet as this moment—"

"Are you done now?" Bauchelain interrupted. "Excellent. Now, good Scribe, perhaps the other prisoner as well?"

"No!" snarled Warmet. "He cheats!"

The other prisoner weakly lifted his head. "Oh," he quailed, "so not fair."

Shrugging, Bauchelain turned to his manservant. "By this, Mister Reese, we see the true breadth of honest compassion, extending no more than a single blessed hair from one's own body, no matter its state. Upon the scene we can ably take measure, indeed, of the world's strait, and if one must, at times, justify the tenets of tyranny, over which a reasonable soul may assert decent propriety over lesser folk, in the name of the threat of terror, then upon solid ground we stand."

"Aye, Master. Solid ground. Standing."

Bauchelain then nodded to Warmet. "We happily yield this keep to you, sir, for as long as you may wish to haunt it, and by extension, the villagers below."

"Most kind of you," Warmet replied.

"Mister Reese."

"Master?"

"Upon this very night, we shall take our leave. Korbal prepares the carriage."

"What carriage?" the manservant asked.

Bauchelain waved a dismissive hand.

Warmet slowly climbed to his feet. Coingood rushed to help him. "See, milord?" he said. "See how worthy I am?"

Warmet grimaced with what few teeth he had left.

"Worthy? Oh indeed, Scribe. Fear not. I am not my brother."

As the sorcerer and his manservant made their way to the steep, stone stairs leading up the ground level, Warmet loosed a low, evil laugh.

Both men turned.

Warmet shrugged. "Sorry. It was a just a laugh."

"Tiny never gets lost," said Tiny, looking around with a frown on his broad, flat brow. The sun was carving its way through the heavy clouds on the horizon. Then he pointed. "There! See!"

The keep's tower was perhaps a third of a league to the south. The brothers set out. Midge, Puny and Scant, and of course Tiny himself. A short time later, after crossing a number of denuded, sandy hills, passing near a wretched shack with thin smoke drifting from its chimney, they reached the track they had, somehow, missed last night.

At the keep's gate they found Relish sitting near a heap that consisted of one corpse lying atop another, with both heads caved in by weapon blows. Their sister rose upon seeing them. "You useless twits," she said. "I saw what was left of the tavern, and Feloovil was wearing a shroud and didn't want to cook me any breakfast."

"Be quiet," Tiny retorted. He walked up to the door and kicked at it.

"It's open," Relish replied.

"Tiny don't use his hands." He kicked again.

Puny walked past and opened the heavy door. They all trooped inside.

They found servants huddled in the stables, their eyes wide and full of fear, and in the house itself there was little to see, barring a pair of broken iron statues lying in murky pools of some foul oily liquid, and the exploded body of some man in robes, lying in the dining hall with demonic footprints stamped in the man's own blood around the corpse.

"We'll have to search every room," Puny said, "and see what's been squirreled away, or who's hiding."

Tiny grunted, glaring about. "The bastards fled. I can feel it. We're not finished with them. Not a chance. Tiny never finishes with anything."

"Look!" cried Scant. "Cookies!" And he and Puny rushed to the table.

From the dirty window, Birds Mottle had watched the Chanters walk past in the pale light of early dawn, and once they were out of sight she sighed and turned back to study Hordilo where he lay on the bed. "Well," she said, "I'm heading into Spendrugle."

"What for?" he demanded.

"I'm tired of this. I'm tired of you, in fact. I never want to see you again."

"If that's what you think," he retorted, "then go on, y'damned gull-smeared cow!"

"I'd rather sleep with a goat," she said, reaching for her weapon belt.

"We was never married, you know," Hordilo said. "I was just using you. Marriage is for fools and I'm no fool. You think I believed you last night? I didn't. I saw you eyeing that goat on the way here."

"What goat?"

"You don't fool me, woman. There ain't a woman in the whole world who can fool me."

"I suppose not," she said, on her way out.

Down in Spendrugle she found the rest of the squad, and there was much rejoicing, before they all headed off to plunder the wreck of the *Suncurl*.

Feeling turgid and sluggish, Ackle walked into the tavern, whereupon he paused and looked round. "Gods, what happened here? Where is everyone?"

From the bar, Feloovil lifted a head to show him a smudged, blotchy face and red eyes. "All dead," she said.

"I always knew it was catching," Ackle replied.

"Come on in and have yourself a drink."

"Really? Even though I'm dead, too?"

Feloovil nodded. "Why not?"

"Thank you!"

"So," she said as she drew out an ale from the tap, "where's that tax collector hiding?"

"Oh, he's not hiding," Ackle said. "He's dead, too."

Feloovil held up the tankard. "Now," she smiled, "that's something we can both drink to."

And so they did.

A little while later Ackle looked round and shivered. "I don't know, Feloovil. It's quiet as a grave in here."

On the road wending north, away from the coast, the massive, black-lacquered carriage rolled heavily, leaf-springs wincing over stones and ruts. The team of six black horses steamed in the chill morning air, and their red eyes flared luminously in the growing light.

For a change, Bauchelain sat beside Emancipor as he worked the traces.

"Such a fine morning, Mister Reese."

"Aye, Master."

"A most enlightening lesson, wouldn't you say, on the nature of tyranny? I admit, I quite enjoyed myself."

"Aye, Master. Why we so heavy here? This carriage feels like a ship with a bilge full of water."

"Ah, well, we are carrying the stolen treasure, so it is no wonder, is it?"

Emancipor grunted around his pipe. "Thought you and Korbal didn't care much for wealth and all that."

"Only as a means to an end, Mister Reese, as I believe I explained last night. That said, since our ends are of much greater value and significance than what might be concocted by a handful of outlawed sentries, well, the course ahead is obvious, wouldn't you say?"

"Obvious, Master. Aye. Still, can't help but feel sorry for that squad."

"In this, Mister Reese, your capacity for empathy shames humankind."

"Heh! And see where it's got me!"

"How churlish of you, Mister Reese. You are very well paid, and taken care of with respect to your many needs, no matter how insipid they might be. I must tell you: you, sir, are the first of my manservants to have survived for as long as you have. Accordingly, I look upon you with con-siderable confidence, and not a little affection."

"Glad to hear it, Master. Still"—he glanced across at

207

Bauchelain—"what happened to all those other manser-vants you had?"

"Why, I had to kill them, each and every one. Despite considerable investment on my part, I might note. Highly frustrating, as you might imagine. And indeed, on a number of occasions, I was in fact forced to defend my-self. Imagine, one's own seemingly loyal manservant at-tempting to kill his master. This is what the world has come to, Mister Reese. Is it any wonder that I envisage a brighter future, one where I sit secure upon a throne, rul-ing over millions of wretched subjects, and immune to all concerns over my own safety? This is the tyrant's dream, Mister Reese."

"I was once told that dreams are worthy things," said Emancipor, "even if they end up in misery and unend-ing horror."

"Ah, and who told you that?"

He shrugged. "My wife."

The open road stretched ahead, a winding track of dislodged cobbles, frozen mud, and on all sides, the day brightened with an air of optimism.

Bauchelain then leaned back and said, "Behold, Mis-ter Reese, this new day!"

"Aye, Master. New day."